She rose and took up her lyre. The sky, what scraps she could see through the treetops, glowed more blue than any sky she had ever seen. The ferns were greener than green. The muted tree trunks sparkled with hidden colors. The lyre in her hands shone, and with a dazzle of insight she saw its nature: the beast that had lived and provided the rib, shaped just so; the inspired spinner of silver, who had drawn out the strings. But its maker she could not see, only two hands, pale of skin, small and strong, that smoothed and stretched and tuned.

She did not realize that she was seeing this new world through eyes that were also new. She walked now with the confidence of a queen in her own realm, and the music that her hand brought from the lyre was as patterned and precise as the cycles of the stars . . .

ARDATH MAYHAR

RUNES OF THE LYRE

ACE FANTASY BOOKS
NEW YORK

This Ace Fantasy Book contains the complete
text of the original hardcover edition.

RUNES OF THE LYRE

An Ace Fantasy Book / published by arrangement with
Atheneum

PRINTING HISTORY
Atheneum edition / 1982
Ace edition / November 1983

ISBN: 0-441-73690-4

Ace Fantasy Books are published by The Berkley Publishing Group,
200 Madison Avenue, New York, New York 10016.
PRINTED IN THE UNITED STATES OF AMERICA

To Valerie,
who cares . . .

Contents

Prologue

THE PLANET hung, seemingly alone, in its wide orbit about a solitary star. No companion lighted its cycles. Only the distant suns of other systems sprinkled its skies with faint glimmers.

Yet it was not as lonely as it seemed. Interlocked with it were invisible worlds that existed in dimensions different from that in which it swung. Each of those worlds was distinctly individual. Some were rock, some ice, some molten magma. One of them was similar to its tangential world. It was called Ranuit.

Ranuit was a huge world. Two immense continents shared its watery surface, though one was much larger than the other. The larger of the two showed signs and traces of human activities—or those of beings like humans. Scars showed whitely, where cities had been burned away with nuclear fires. Stone structures, more primitive than the ruins, marked areas where living beings were in residence. Vast stretches of forest patched the temperate zones of that continent, and its deep-green cloak was decorated with a few large farming complexes.

It was obvious, had there been an observer, that a growing culture lived on that continent, occupying itself with the things that most sentient beings always attend to: feeding itself, supplying luxuries to a few and labor to many.

The other continent was quite different. Its forest

stretched from end to end, seemingly without artificial breaks in its expanse. Yet that landmass was pinched narrow in the north, widened only slightly in the temperate zone. It was in the tropical latitudes (for that planet possessed a tilted axis) that its forest became rampant—even triumphant.

And among the tremendous boles of the trees, had one swooped low to see, could be found jewellike patterns that resolved themselves into dwellings roofed with blossom and leaf, pools persuaded to seem natural, yet shaped and deepened with artful grace.

Among those gemmed domiciles lived a people so old in wisdom and perception that they seemed almost other than human. They alone, of all the waking population of Ranuit, understood the relation of their world to that other, central planet, which to its own people was known as the Heart of the Worlds.

Only those people of the forest were aware that beneath a tower, in a ruined city across the waters of their own planet, time was ticking away toward the moment when those who had all but shattered Ranuit once before would wake again. They knew. They feared. They watched in two dimensions as a desperate venture commenced to unfold.

It began almost innocently . . .

The Rune
of the Key

I

I<small>T HUNG</small> in the willows. Its greenbone frame blended so finely with the trailing fronds that the eye could not find it, and the ear was astonished to hear its thin lament as the wind fingered its strings. Its shape was that of a crescent moon, though the lower horn curled outward in a pleasing arc, ready for the hand to hold.

It swung lightly in the morning breeze, and the shallow stream that threaded among the willow boles sang counterpoint to its voice. As the sun rose higher, and the streams of summer burned away, a cicada added its voice. The many small things in the grasses of the streambank skreeked and shimmered above all.

In the forenoon there came a sudden silence. A footfall, muffled by the summer dusts, came padding down the path that flanked the stream. Young frogs leaped hysterically into the pools as the sound neared them, and the translucent green water snakes curled lazily from sight into the reeds.

A current of air stirred the willows, and the lyre hummed its minor note.

Two green eyes searched upward, and a curved mouth curved more widely when the eyes found the hanging shape of the instrument in the branches. As easily as would a child or a cat, the girl swung into the willow tree and climbed surefootedly up the slanting trunk. Slithering along a limb, she stretched a slender arm to its fullest extension and hooked the lyre from its place.

With the careless grace of the young, she dropped from the tree, her ragged-petaled skirts blooming wide about her. There in the dust of the greeny-shadowed path, she examined the instrument carefully, drawing from distant memory the recollection of a minstrel who wandered about a torchlit hall with just such a thing clasped to his shoulder.

He had held it just so . . . and she caught the lower curve in her left hand, tucked the bow into her shoulder, and touched the strings with nervous fingers. Though by rights the lyre should have been slack-stringed, if not worse, after hanging for an unmeasured time in a willow tree, the notes she struck were clear and pure. The scale that followed her questing finger from front to back was as true as the notes from the stream beside her.

Chuckling with delight, she caught up her ragged bundle from the spot where it had dropped, hung it across her shoulder by a much-mended cord, and set off again to follow the winding water. Though days of deerlike caution lay behind her, she dared, now and again, to pluck from her newfound toy a shower of notes. Yet even so, after each attempt at music, she stood for a moment, listening intently, her head cocked toward her backtrail. Still, she seemed fearless, standing in her outworn and all but outgrown frock, her feet bare to the comfort of the warm dust, her arms and legs scratched as if by flight, and the fading marks of old scars on her apricot-tinted cheeks.

Never was there hint nor sign of any follower, and she grew bolder in her experimenting with the new toy. Once . . . once, indeed, she had been taught to play the lyre. Almost, the memory was lost in the chaos that lay between this time and that. Nevertheless, the old lessoning began to return to her as she walked, eyes ever searching ahead, feet following the animal path beside the stream.

A quaver of unsure music drifted from the lyre. An old nursery tune. For an instant a wrinkled and rosy face stood in the eye of her memory, together with the steamy smell of good soup, the rubbing of big rough towels, the secure crispness of a clean bed. Then it was gone, and the little song died away.

Suddenly she lifted her head, and a roguish expression appeared in her green eyes. Tossing a gypsy-tangle of black curls away from her cheek, she picked out a sprightly jig that had been the only music at her last stopping place. Not home. Home had been a tall house of stone, ringed with walls that had seemed, to her infant mind, to reach the sky. Home was lost in a turmoil of smoke and screams and clashing metal and a rough hand that had swept her from beneath horse hooves to the dubious security of a saddle.

Still, except for the lechery of the master, the last place that had given her haven had been a fair one. The jig rang out beneath her fingers, true and rhythmic. Her feet took up the beat, skipping along the path in a series of intricate steps. What matter if the rude old man of Indris might be following to drag her, all unwilling, to his bed? The sun was warm, the shadows were cool, she had caught a fish in the dawnlight to stay her belly's pangs. Now she danced.

The sun swung down, and tree shadow lengthened across her way. The purling of the stream became deeper-noted as it widened and deepened. The willows were older and bigger. Their gray shapes leaned over the stream like peaked bridges, for they met in its middle, some of them. Now she walked wearily, quiet and again hungry.

Her fingers once more sought the strings of the lyre. A sad wisp of melody wandered the way before her, losing itself in the darkening tunnel of the path. Gaining confidence, she drew from the harp a hint of the pain of her losses, the bitterness of her wanderings since the one who had saved her, from the ruins his own kind had made of her home, had died in another battle. She had grieved because he had been kind, though he had not really known how to be with a terrified five-year-old.

Ahead of her, among the willows, at a point where the forest merged with the path's gray outriders, something formed in the shadowy air. The wine-cool evening flowed through an opening that had not been there before the notes had found the spot. There was a scent there, not of cool waters laced with living things and forest resined with spring, but of dry and tangy uplands. Yet the opening seemed, now, to be only an arch leading into a berry thicket arbor roofed with tangled vines.

The sun was long lost behind the trees when she

reached that place. An eddy that pooled at the root of one of the willows promised good fishing, and she dropped her bundle, put the lyre carefully atop it, and lay on her stomach beside the stream. Dark shapes hung motionless below the surface, and she slipped her hands into the water, one to her right, the other to her left, making no slightest sound as she did so. Of the lessons she had learned from lost Arbold, this was the most valuable.

Her slender hands wavered through the water, slowly, casually, as though they, too, lived and had business there. Then, with one swift motion, they came together and emerged, clasping a wildly flopping trout.

Fire was a luxury she had forsaken. Though she had no assurance that those of Indris hunted her, she knew with the certainty of a child or an animal that the old man would not let her escape without a search.

She looked about for a hidden spot in which to eat her raw and squirming repast. The arched opening into the thorny thicket beckoned, and she took up her bundle and slipped between the stickery branches and sharp-toothed vines. Inside the arborlike spot there was open ground covered with short grasses. Angle-branched hawthorn walled it securely.

With a tired sigh, she dropped her bundle and sat flat on the cool earth. Killing her fish neatly with the stolen kitchen knife that lived in a sling of cord at her waist, she opened it and stripped out the blood-stippled white meat. Though in the ten years of her wanderings she had eaten more raw food than cooked, it had never become easy for her. She closed her eyes, swallowed hard, then began to chew the meat.

As she ate, she tried to think of anything except what she was doing. She gazed upward at the stooping bushes and woven vines. She felt and enjoyed the coolness against her legs as she stretched them before her. She smelled, even over the scent of the fish, a fresh and tangy atmosphere unlike any she knew and tried to imagine where it came from. Swallowing the last of the fish, she wiped her hands and mouth on a taggle of skirt and sniffed hard. Something like sun-dried grass. Dusty stone. A faint fragrance that suggested furtive and half-dried blossoms. And, distantly, faintly, but clearly, an enchanting fragrance that must be trees—a forest of them—but trees unlike any in the lush wood beside her.

A little breeze came from deeper in the hideaway, and she lifted her pack and wriggled into the tangle, following it. At its deepest extent, a fallen tree made an angle with the bole of a warped trunk. From this mouthlike opening the breeze danced forth in lively vigor.

She moved through and looked out into a world she couldn't recognize. Across a dizzying gulf of space she could see a distant forest. Mountains were visible, curving to right and to left. She shivered at the alienness of the scene and started to scutter back to the safety of her known, though still perilous, world. Then she stopped and rubbed her nose. The green eyes lit with curiosity.

Surely the old man of Indris could never find her there! A surge of excitement pulsed through her. The

adventurous spirit that had not been subdued by her hard
life moved her forward, dragging her bundle behind her,
into the new world that opened from the thicket. She
stood, looked around her, and almost staggered. Before
her was a sheer drop to distant grassland. And she had
stepped, seemingly, out of solid stone!

At her back was a cliff face that overhung the steep
slope on which she stood. Before her was a slanting drop
of many hundreds of feet—perhaps thousands. Her experience had lain in gently rolling country, and she had
no yardstick by which to measure the tremendous
reaches that lay there.

The spot on which her feet rested was ledgelike,
but its outer edge was an angle, not a sheer drop. A
prickly sort of bush grew from a crack in the stone beside her, and at its base, thrusting outward, then up, was
a clump of gray-silver weed whose tiny violet flowers
provided a dry-sweet fragrance to the cool evening air.
The sun, almost below the edge of the earth, was long
lost in this sharp-peaked place, but its last warm rays
struck towering crags to her right and left with rose-
golden fires.

Down the slope lay cool blue and purple shadow, and
deep within that shade was a deeper one that she knew
must be the forest whose scent had drawn her from her
own world. She was in a *new* world. She laid her hand
on the warm face of the rock behind her and laughed.
No son of Indris was likely to find her here! She struck
a triumphant chord on the lyre, and at the other side

of that doorway between dimensions, the air rippled, and a portal was gone.

II

There was no path to ease her way downward. Crosspaths there were, many of them, and she glimpsed traces of small and knife-edged hoofprints and dried droppings that told of denizens of these high places. None went toward the forest, though its clean and intoxicating tang filled all the air. As the sky darkened, the chill of the heights was filled with it, and she hurried the last of the way down.

There was no easing of the dividing line between the height and the forested ways. Straight and tall as the wall of her father's keep stood the first rank of trees; great, gray-brown boled firs that peaked in a whispering roof a hundred feet above the root-clenched soil. It was night among those corridors, and the sounds of hunting beasts were already beginning to chitter and squawk and growl in the deeps.

The girl had spent much of her short life in forest, though a far different sort from this. She knew well the dangers that night might bring to one unsheltered and unarmed. And those straight columns rose, unbranched, a dozen yards above her head, too thick for six men to span with linked hands and outstretched arms. She knew that there could be no shinnying up such giants.

Looking longingly back, now and again, she retraced her steps to a place where an ugly gnome of a rock stood alone at the base of the cliff. Twice the height of a cottage, lumpy and flat-topped, it seemed the most nearly secure spot that she might find in this new land. After a few tries, she managed to fling the bundle onto it, without having it fall back into her face. The lyre she dared not treat so roughly, but she had no intention of abandoning it, so she untied her knife cord and looped it through the back of the curve, carefully arranging the strings to extend outward to avoid damage from her movements.

It was no difficult climb. Only twice did she need to rely on fingertips and dug-in toes to sustain her weight against a sheer spot. Only once did she trust her fate to the fickle gods and swing by one hand around protruding knobs of rock. Always she found herself, whole and undamaged, at the spot at which she had aimed herself.

The top was, indeed, flattish, though it had a pronounced list on its downhill side. There was even a low ridge against which she huddled to avoid the cool winds that moved down from the heights. Digging into her bundle, she drew forth a fragment of woolen blanket, her sole legacy from Arbold, and wrapped it about herself. As the darkness drew together into one seamless fabric of blackness, she caught the lyre once more into the curve of her arm and touched its strings.

A tenuous ripple of sound rose from the rock. Almost, the invisible trees seemed to stiffen with shock. The multitudinous business of the forest was silenced in one breath. The sound moved outward in a swift circle, and in its wake it left stillness and amazement. A tingle of strangeness filled the places that it left behind.

Unaware upon her rock, the girl harkened back and back to the music that had been a part of her days, long ago. Some part of her aloneness, a great deal of her hurt found their way into the notes that she now brought from her instrument. A haunting strain filled the night and moved away across the wood. Tensions built within the fabric of this new world that threatened lightnings and thunders.

Then she slept, but her music moved still, into places of which its maker had never dreamed. Beyond the wood, the charged stillness woke strange things in the forest. Watchers who had slept for years opened their eyes from long rest, called again to the world of the living by notes of power sprung from a hand whose authority had long been missing from their world. Neryi, Child of the Asyi, looked southward for the first time in many lives of shorter-lived men, and a stirring of hope moved within his heart.

III

The sun, sidling past the southward mountains, woke the girl. For a time she lay still, thinking of the events of the day before, checking her surroundings to make certain that she was, indeed, where she thought. But the wood still loomed downhill, the conical fir tops piercing, it seemed, the intensely blue sky. In the morning light the meadow edge was starred with small yellow blossoms, above which pale blue butterflies dipped and hovered.

The hem of the wood glowed with the first slanting of the sun, the huge boles glowing golden-umber in the newly minted rays.

No terror lived there now, and low-growing greenery hinted at possible sources of food, which again had become an immediate problem.

She bundled her scanty belongings and flung the pack to the ground. Attaching the lyre to her knife cord, she slipped a seeking toe down the rockface, found a niche, and went down swiftly.

She found the forest to be a place of strange beauty. Used to the vine-tangled lushness of the low-country woods, she marveled at the clean and needled floor of this new sort of place. Patches and strips of fern and three-leaved flowers grew where rifts in the distant tree-tops let through the sun. In these she hunted, grubbing up roots, rubbing away the light loam to see them, smell them, and finally to taste one or two that seemed promising. But the flavor was appalling, and she spat and spat and finally vomited a bit, though her empty inside gave up nothing but fluid.

For almost two weeks there had been only what food she could forage for herself, fish and berries and a hare caught in a forgotten snare. Even those temporary havens that turned, always, into traps had provided enough scraps of bread and meat to sustain her life and growth, but now her green eyes were beginning to seem entirely too large for the pale oval of her face. Weariness, a thing she had seldom known, was becoming a constant companion. Fear, which she thought to be lost with her childhood, was tapping at the back door of her mind.

Still, Arbold had been, in his rough way, the best teacher for one who was to be tossed into the world to make her way unaided. She knew many things that secure folk have no need to learn. The discipline that survival imposes was a part of her backbone. She observed acutely, though unconsciously, everything about her surroundings. She thought before she acted. And now she turned her face down into the depths of the forest. Behind her was nothing to sustain her. Before might lie death, in very truth, but she would die, as had Arbold, in the act of living, if that became necessary.

The walking was easy, the path cushioned with a pad of needles as deep as the roots, almost, and as old as the forest itself. Flashes of scarlet and sun-yellow and emerald flitted from tree to tree, and the trilling comments of the bright birds accompanied her on her way. Her heart lifted, and to drown out the complaints of her stomach, she crooked her arm about the lyre again and played the lilting melody to which, in those half-forgotten days, her father's folk had danced among the rushes in the stone-floored hall.

As she played, the forest stilled as if congealed within a topaz. No bird moved or lifted its voice. No small beast scurried through ferns. Unaware, she raised her young voice, clear and true for all its lack of training, and crooned a wordless accompaniment to the notes of the lyre.

She walked through a frozen forest, all unknowing, and the serpent among the ferns was rigid in his coil, as her bare feet passed by. The she-bear saw her pass and could not roar with rage. The very breeze stilled in the branches overhead, and no whisper interrupted her music.

The Watchers, now alert in every fiber, looked always toward the forest and the mountains beyond. When the clear morning light began to dance upon a vast but invisible bubble that spanned the wood, Neryi rose from his gleaming ivory chair and set a lens into a frame. Through it he looked, frowning.

He saw a strange thing. It was very like a bubble, indeed, catching the light of the sky and the sun and rippling them in quivering rainbows over all its domed surface. The treetops within it were visible, though slightly distorted.

He laid his thumb against a gem that was one of many, blue and ruby and topaz, set into a circle upon his wall. Within his mind, a voice spoke.

"Wonder of wonders!" it said. "Do the Children of the Asyi deign to notice their short-lived cousins?" The sardonic note was not lost on him who had called, and his tawny face stilled with irritation. Yet he answered civilly, his golden eyes never leaving the wood and its encompassing bubble.

"Neryi, Watcher to the South. Yestereve a troubling ran through the lands. It woke us of the Asyi from our long sleep. Today the forest over against the mountains is domed within a bubble that ripples with light. Nothing stirs there that my lens can discern. I feel no danger, yet there is unease within me. Can it be, think you—"

The voice interrupted him. "—that a Key has re-entered Hasyih? That Notes of Power are even now being played within the wood? That old granny tales hold something of truth after all? I think not. We who do not spend our time in sleep have disproved all the old nonsense. Yet I shall send to the forest, if only in celebration of the awakening of the Children of the Asyi. Such an event is worthy of some special effort." The voice was almost openly laughing.

Neryi removed his thumb from the ruby, and the voice was gone. His mouth twisted ruefully as he returned his attention to the encased wood. It was an indication of a malaise that must have been growing in Hasyih, he mused, that a mere technician would feel secure in subtly mocking a Watcher, one of the Children of the Asyi. To mock, as well, the traditions that were the foundation of the Heart of the Worlds. And to mention the Key in a tone of amused contempt was indication that the sickness had gone deep, in the span of his own tranced sleep. Surely, Those Who Pattern the Worlds must have slept also, to allow such slackness to creep into the Heart of the Worlds.

The day moved smoothly over the dome of the forest, and the play of rippling rainbow changed as the light changed. But the Key that must, indeed, be once again within the realm did not release its field. Neryi knew that any forces the technician might send would not find the old paths open to them.

"A Key may unlock—and also lock," he mused aloud, as the sun slipped behind the heights to the west. The long twilight grayed the lands and smoothed the bubble to mother-of-pearl. When its last touch had followed the sun over the mountains and darkness encompassed all Hasyih, Neryi looked upon the forest with awe. For now the bubble was a webbing of golden motes, burning in the night.

A jewel glowed emerald, and he touched it with his thumb. The voice was no longer sardonic. Now it was frightened.

"Power blooms upon our border, Neryi! The Silliyi that I sent were unable to enter the wood, try as they might. And now that terrible glow fills them with fear. Even those of the City look southward with strong lenses and see that unnatural light. Can it be . . . can it be that there is truth in the myths we were told as children?"

Neryi laughed and did not try to conceal his laughter. "Now you seek out the Children of the Asyi, Ayilli, with a somewhat different tone. If you were taught of the Keys as myths, of the burden that lies upon Hasyih as the Heart of the Worlds, even of the Queen Who Is to Come, as mere tales to dry the tears of children, surely our race has slipped backward from the high place in which Those Who Pattern the Worlds placed it. You of short lives know and conceal from yourselves the knowledge that the Children of the Asyi exist. That we live many multiples of your spans of life. That we sleep for centuries, when we are unneeded, and wake for centuries more, when we are called to action. You pretend that we are something of no more consequence than those who guard the Empty Tower. Yet when there is danger or even mere strangeness you call upon us and panic is in your voice."

There was no answer, and Neryi said, bitterly, "You fear for your brief lives. Yet what, I wonder, have you ever done to earn even those terms of existence? Even in our sleep, we know of your lusts and your cruelties. A day will come, Ayilli, when you and your kind will be called to account."

The emerald glow winked out, and Neryi sighed with annoyance at his outburst. He well knew, with all his rare kindred, that one could not reason with the short-lived people.

With one last glance at the enwebbed forest, he sank into his deep chair and linked minds with his brothers and sisters. Not through the use of coarse material things like the gems did the Children of the Asyi join together their consciousnesses, but through tendrils of Power that sang out through the air of Hasyih. Close-knit in that tenuous webbing, the six Children of the Asyi took counsel.

IV

For all her stoutness of heart, the girl grew wary as the day waned. Though she had seen no moving creature in all her day's walk through the forest, she had heard the muted roars and growls of the night before, and she knew that large beasts tenanted the place. Still, there was no refuge to be found. Not a single tree had shown to her a diseased spot that promised a hollow and safety. No branch was within reach, no bole small enough to clamber up.

She played the lyre softly now and only when she needed to keep her courage at hand. Something in its pure voice gave comfort. And comfort was sorely needed as the shadows became total blackness, forcing her to stop and to huddle against a tree trunk, wrapped again in her scrap of wool.

Then she chanced to look up, and her eyes grew wide with wonder. Netted in the treetops were a thousand thousand fireflies of light. They cast no gleam upon the forest floor, but they hung in glimmering splendor against the patches of sky-blackness and tree-blackness, and her fear vanished.

Still the forest was gripped in its frozen state. No pad of paw nor growl of hunting beast sounded in all its reaches, and the notes of the lyre hung above and greeted their sisters the stars. The girl slept against the tree, the lyre clutched in her arms, and not even an untoward dream ventured near her.

She woke cramped and stiff, the instrument still held tightly. Knowing as she was in the ways of forests, she was a bit surprised to wake at all, but she did not question her good fortune. She merely bundled her belongings again and set out, holding the dawnlight at her right. A hundred paces along her way she paused and looked carefully at a patch of mushrooms.

Many times she had been cautioned by Arbold.

"Better to starve," he had grunted, "then to die in agony. Eat no fungus that you know less well than your right hand."

But her young inside was now ravenous, and the cramping pains went through all her body. These were innocent-seeming enough, she thought, being creamy-white and palely dotted upon their tops with tan. Surely, in all this expanse of forest, there must be some edible thing to fill her stomach.

She weighed the decision for a moment. Then, with the optimism of youth and inexperience, she took up one of the buttons that had just pushed through the mold and nibbled a bit off the side. It had a yeasty taste, not unpleasant. When a short time had passed, she ventured a bite. Then, having no problem that she could detect, she fell upon the patch and ate her fill.

Satisfied at last, she rose and took up her burdens. The sky, what scraps she could see through infrequent gaps in the treetops, glowed more blue than any sky she had ever seen. The ferns were greener than green, and their curling fronds of new growth seemed edged in gold. The muted tree trunks sparkled with hidden colors, only now to be seen and reveled in. The lyre in her hands shone even more greenly than did the wood, and with a dazzle of insight she saw its nature: the beast that had lived and provided the rib, shaped just so; the inspired spinner of silver, who had drawn out the strings from his molten store. But its maker she could not see, only two hands, pale of skin, small and strong, that smoothed and stretched and tuned.

She did not realize that she was seeing this new world through eyes that were also new, or that the mushrooms she had eaten had changed her vision together with her thought. Even her face was changed. Her green eyes now held a spark of something strange, and the set of her chin was firmer and less girlish than it had been when she woke. She walked now with the confidence of a queen within her own realm, and the music that her hand brought from the lyre was as patterned and precise as the cycles of the stars.

She came to the farther edge of the forest in the warm light of afternoon. The meadows that ran to the very foot of the wood glowed with wind-rippled grasses and small bright flowers and darting dragonflies that were enameled in every hue the eye could detect. Upon a triumphant chord, she stepped from the forest into the meadow's grass.

Behind her there was a thin hum of tension, then a crack like lightning. There was a gust of sound, chirps and trills, squawks and screams and growls and roars and chirrupings of every sort imaginable. The forest woke from its stasis, and every creature within it cried out in an agony of release and . . . loss.

She stood for a moment, and the new thing within her knew what had happened within the forest. With a quiet nod, she moved into the meadow, her eyes fixed now upon a glint of metal in the grass ahead.

Her fingers, as she walked through grasses that bowed before her in the wind as if to do homage, strayed across the strings. An intricate webbing of sound strung itself throughout the meadow, stilling even those Sil-liyi who were still conscious. Those in the grass, bright figures in silver armor that would have amused a true soldier, sank even more deeply into trance. Only the silken fringes of a bright tent (set in the midst of a ring of fallen men) moved to the handling of the breeze.

So she came, the nameless girl from a world adjacent to Hasyih, into the place to which the lyre was the Key. Standing before the silent tent, she looked down at Ayilli, sprawled in his ensorcellment, and the eyes that could now see things to their sources and their true selves scanned him swiftly. Her lip curled as she looked.

A bright thread of sound splintered the silence. Away to the north she could see moving things, glints of silver and brass. The thrumming of hooves vibrated under her feet. The lyre in her hands seemed to tremble eagerly in response to the call of the horn, and she tucked it closer and touched the strings.

Turning her back upon Ayilli and his men, she walked out upon the blossom-starred grass, clouds of butterflies swirling about her feet like a strange-colored mist. She struck the lyre one crashing chord, and the sound rang like a challenge or a greeting across the distances, and in the next moment it mingled with the thin, sweet tenor of the horn. Again the world froze, the sky like porcelain, the grass like enamel, the insects like painted things upon a wall, motionless in midair.

Only she moved and they who were coming moved, crossing the distances between them.

When they met, she stood proudly and looked at the

tawny-golden men and women, three of each, who sat creamy steeds and looked down at her with awe and reverence. Then Neryi dropped from his horse and knelt.

His kindred did likewise, wonder dawning in their eyes, as he bent his proud head until his forehead touched the grass at her feet.

"We are most blessed," he said, rising again. "Our generation has seen the coming of the Queen again into Hasyih."

The girl's brow wrinkled, and her green eyes grew confused. "I?" she asked. "I am no queen . . . I think . . . I have come through a strange door through stone. I have seen and heard things unlike those in my own world. Yet I cannot tell you my father's name or the name of his tall keep that lies now in ruin. I cannot tell you my own name, for it was lost when Arbold took me away on his horse. I have been 'child.' I have been 'girl.' I have not been what the old man of Indris called me, but only because I ran away."

"You are Yinri," said Neryi firmly. "Only you could have used the lyre to wake us, to enspell the forest, for it goes only to the one whose time it is to partake of its power. I can see in your eyes that you have eaten the food of the forest. No one can eat it and live except those of the line of the Queen Who Is to Come. You are the link that will bind us again to those short-lived cousins whose need called you forth from an alien dimension.

"And we are those whose task it has been to wait. We are more fortunate than our fathers, or theirs, for we have seen the end of waiting. Come Yinri, Queen of Hasyih. The Empty Tower is waiting, even now."

V

There was a horse for her. Not creamy, like those of the Asyi, but gleaming black, trapped in emerald. Neryi whirled her up in one easy swing, and she sat, looking down at him and his kin, her hands gripping the lyre. Something was happening inside her. It continued to happen, even as they all rode away toward the city. Vast patterns were moving together within her, making coherent wholes whose outlines were still alien to her mind. Rivers of knowledge seemed to break free of their bounds and to course through the runnels of her brain, and she felt fit to drown in the flood of knowledge.

Still they rode, as the night rolled out from the east before them. Though the horses must be walked and rested, the Asyi seemed anxious at the loss of time. Yet with iron control they tended their steeds' requirements, while their own inclinations still pounded on eastward at undiminished pace.

At last, in a time of walking and leading the horses, the girl spoke to Neryi, who was always at her left shoulder, afoot or ahorse.

"What do you fear, Neryi of the Asyi? Why such haste? Can it be that something is amiss within your city?"

He grunted and swung again into his saddle. "Much is amiss," he said, as she mounted and they moved out at a brisk walk. "We of the Asyi sleep for spans of years, and your notes woke us to anxiety. Much has happened in the years since our last awakening, and most of it is ill, we fear. The short-lived have lost the truth of their history and their teachings. They have fallen into error. And worse. Those who slept in the meadow—Ayilli and his Silliyi—have grown insolent, even with the Children of the Asyi. They are, with their fellows yonder in the city, a peril . . . to us and to you, and even, in their ignorance and arrogance, to themselves.

"We ride swiftly because we fear that when Ayilli wakes, if he has not already done so, he will rouse his fellows within the city against us. They have no wish, those whose lives are measured in decades, to see the Coming of the Queen."

Then they trotted, and no other word was spoken, as the solid shape of the city rose before them from the dark of the meadows against the lesser darkness of the spangled sky. But the girl, who was now, indeed, Yinri, seemed to see it as it would be on a fair afternoon with the mellow light of the westering sun turning the walls to antique gold and lighting scarlet roofs and tower tops to bright conflagration. Some memory not her own had seen it thus, and it was poured into her mind so that she, too, might see it.

A hard shiver shook her. Somewhere within her, the child that she had been only a day before cried forlornly, shut away into a closet that had no window. A harder and more sophisticated mind had seated itself at the reins of her spirit. The tough skills of her mind and body were welcome additions to the formidable armory of ability the new self had brought with it, but she felt her young self being relentlessly quenched.

Still, she felt no true regret. Her life was not one upon which she might look back with wistfulness. Behind her lay hardship and hunger and whips and the backs of hands. Not since Arbold had any tried to aid or to comfort her. Now it seemed that she had six, at least, who set themselves at her service. And before her lay a city and a tower that were her own, if Neryi could be believed.

So she said no more, but rode tirelessly with the Asyi until they were under a black wall that loomed against the stars as had the forest before the mountains. That wall was tall, and one could feel its great thickness.

When they stopped beneath its lowering bulk, she whispered, "Why, in this mountain-ringed place, is there need for a wall at all? What enemy could come against Hasyih?"

"Hasyih manufactures her own enemies . . . within," came an answering murmur. "And yet, at one time, when our most remote ancestors were still unborn, Hasyih was not the Heart of the Worlds, but lay open to comers from all directions. The mountains rose at the command of Those Who Pattern the Worlds. And now the Heart of the Worlds has begun to rot."

"Ah!" sighed Yinri, and she found memories again moving into her mind, filling in detail that Neryi had not mentioned.

The gates were closed, which caused the Asyi to

murmur among themselves. At last Neryi said softly, "They can only be closed against our coming. That being true, it would be folly to hail the guard. We must enter by the old way."

There was a shush of expelled breath about him in the blackness. Then a tentative voice asked, "Know you that way, Brother? Not in the lifetime of any now living, no, nor of our sires, has it been used. We have no knowledge of it."

"I am Eldest," he answered. "It was given to me, with other heavy burdens. Follow, and lead your mounts."

They dismounted and fell into line, placing themselves by whispered instructions. Yinri was just behind Neryi, and she could hear the soft plod of hooves, but no sound of footfall was to be heard. Her own steps were as light, for she had followed Arbold in many dangerous ways and secret flights, and his teaching was habit with her.

She knew that Neryi, lost in the darkness before her, was counting, though how she knew it she could not have said. She followed, and she felt no fear, no doubt of this stranger who had taken her life into his hand. Just so had Arbold done, and she had had no cause to regret it. And now, in one instant of newfound maturity, she realized that neither had Arbold regretted the illogical impulse that had linked her to his picaresque existence.

They had made a strange sort of family. Arbold, solitary by habit and circumstance, had reached out for one human hold upon the world, and she had filled his need as he had filled hers. Their affection had been wordless and without outward sign, but each had known a place in the other's mind and heart.

The footfalls stopped ahead of her, and she automatically followed suit, straining her ears. There was a mumble, all but voiceless, in the darkness. Stone ground painfully against stone, and rusted fittings creaked. Against the black wall an even deeper blackness appeared.

"Come!" Neryi whispered, and she passed that word to the Asyi behind and went into the opening.

It was like being in the womb of the world. The weight of stone lay about and above her. No light, she felt sure, had ever pierced these ways. The sounds they made, the clicking of hooves and the scuff of feet in gravelly dust, were magnified and rolled back at them from ahead and behind. She reached right and left and found that the width of the passage was just sufficient to accommodate a laden beast.

For an instant, there in that tomb of a spot, she stood again on the streambank, looking up through sun-streaked willows at the greenness of the lyre. Even the smell of the lazy waters, the green things that grew in it, the sharp greenness of the willows returned to her. Some compulsion moved within her, and she shifted the lyre into the crook of her arm and touched the strings.

A stately pavane threaded out beneath her fingers, and a chill and silver light grew down the length of the way. Far ahead, she could see the blank-walled end of the passage, where, no doubt, another incantation would make an opening. But the silver light grew stronger, and there came a grating ahead and to the right. Dust shivered into the dead air, dulling the light, and again stone groaned against stone.

Neryi stoped, watching cautiously as the side passage opened. "Lady?" he said tentatively, but she gestured him quiet with a nod and missed no note of her music.

With no word, accepting the validity of her instinct, the Children of the Asyi followed Neryi into the new way. Behind them the stone groaned shut, and the silver light danced away ahead of them, down the grim gray-dusted passage that showed no sign that the foot of man had ever touched it since the last mason put away his trowel. But something moved with them. They all felt it, looking ahead and behind, though nothing could be seen.

"It is only . . . attention," said Neryi, at last. "We are moving with a Pattern, and They have roused to see us."

This was a very long passage, and Yinri, with her new store of knowledge, knew that it moved parallel to the outward wall of the City, spaced between abutting walls of rows of houses. The slight curve that made itself apparent confirmed her belief, but she said nothing. Her hand moved upon the strings with tireless exactitude, and the silver notes spun away down the way, and it seemed that this time would never have an end.

Still, there came an end, at last, in a blank wall of

stone blocks centered with a single slab of sufficient size to admit one person at a time. Yinri sidled past her horse and Neryi's to face the doorway. A shower of patterned notes rained about her.

Soundlessly, easily, the slab moved aside, into the thickness of the wall. There was a darkness beyond that made the dark of the outer passage seem to be only dimness. It purled out into the passage like smoke, and only the silver notes drove it back in again.

She turned to the Children of the Asyi, and her face was that of a furious and mature woman, a queen. "There have been abominations within the temple!" she cried. "Those who were given the trust have betrayed it. Woe to them. Come!" and she stepped into the door.

Thick blackness, like some sick miasma, clogged their throats and their lungs. Yinri, however, seemed untroubled physically, though her anger burned through the clinging abomination like flame. Her hand was busy upon the lyre.

They struggled into the temple, finding their way by old memory and the feel of the paving to their feet. Crowding close about Yinri, the Asyi found that a bubble of clearer air clung about her, so, close-ranked, they came to the center of the great chamber that rose about them in invisible immensity.

Now the notes of the lyre were no longer silver. The making of light was a purpose left behind, it seemed, for a new pattern of chords and rhythms formed. This new music was compelling, demanding, irresistible. Caught in its grip, the Asyi linked hands and minds and wove about the still figure of Yinri a dance of utmost intricacy, though each new measure came directly through feet and bodies and arms without any direction from their minds.

The air grew cleaner. Inch by yard, the tendrils of clinging corruption drew away from the music and the motion. The evil that dwelt in that once-holy place was strangling upon its own wickedness.

Tirelessly Yinri and the Asyi played and danced, note set neatly upon note, foot to floor, hand to hand, mind to mind, without flaw or hesitation. The darkling life that had found place there writhed and retreated, squirmed and shrank, struggled and began to die. Yinri's notes grew triumphant. Like a tremendous bell, the entire temple gonged now with reverberations, and the ugly thing that had been brought to life there was no more.

VI

When the air was pure and clean and wholesome as that of the forest, Yinri halted her hand upon the strings. With a whisper of feet upon dusty floor, the Asyi drifted to stillness. They stood for many heartbeats, silent in the darkness, listening to the repose that had returned to the temple.

There was, at last, a faint chuckle from Neryi. "Do you now have any doubt, Lady, that you are the Queen Who Was to Come?"

With a great sigh, Yinri bent to set the lyre upon the floor. The darkness almost disoriented her, and she caught her breath as the world spun. Instantly a square hand was at her elbow, and Neryi said, "Make light. This is terrible work for one so young. We must see to the Queen."

Footsteps retreated, neat and certain, across the floor, and soon a bubble of golden flame came from a crystal lamp, which hung from chains that disappeared into the deeps of the arched roof. One after another, seven lamps sprang into life, and now the temple was before them, its mosaic floor dusty and betracked, its simple wooden benches stained and cracked. Yet there was a certain awe to the place, now that that alien life was gone from it.

Almost, the hum of ancient chants seemed to echo from its inward-angled walls. The force of ardent belief had charged the wood and the stone for millennia, not to be driven out by a short interlude of blasphemy. Yinri drew herself upright, holding to Neryi's hand, and looked all about her with a sternly measuring gaze.

"It is enough?" she asked Neryi, and he and his brothers and sisters answered together, "Lady, we believe so."

"Then let us be about our work," she said, but Neryi shook his head.

"We must rest, Yinri. You most of all must sleep and gather up your strength. Remember that you are not only Yinri the Queen but also that tender child who walked into the forest, lyre in hand. She must have thought taken for her, too, for she is a part of you, as you are of her. Even we, fresh from our long span of sleep, are again weary and would rest our limbs, though our eyes will not close this night."

Tears rose into the green eyes, and the tangle of dark hair drooped against his shoulder. "Once . . . there were those who cared for me so . . ." she murmured, her lashes dropping shut.

So the Children of the Asyi bore her from the temple into a small chamber where a couch and chairs offered them repose. Neryi laid her upon the couch and smoothed her curls from her cheek, gazing upon her sleeping face with a quizzical expression on his own.

"Will you tell her when she wakes?" asked his sister Amaryi.

"There is much to be done before the old laws and the old traditions may have their day," he answered. "She has a terrible task before her. Why should I bring her, perhaps, distress of mind? The Law will have its day when there is time and space for it. And who knows —we, too, can die, my kindred, as easily as those whose lives are counted in tens, when arrow or blade finds us out. It may be that she need never know."

Amaryi looked him full in the face. Then her lips curved into a tiny smile. "As you say, Neryi. But I think you will regret it, if it happens so."

Then they turned to their own rest, as the dawn outside the temple brightened into a cloudless day. The blast of horns reached them dimly, now and again, and they felt rather than heard the city tremble beneath marching feet. In the chamber where they sat in the light of one dimmed lamp, the Children of the Asyi tightened their lips and hardened their hearts against those whose welfare had been their major concern.

When the girl woke, they were still sitting in the dimness, their eyes bright with pain and determination. For a time Yinri was uncertain, her two halves seeming to make only uneasy accommodation within her single self. But her memory was clear and edged with flame. Purpose brought her up from the couch to stand before her six loyal guides.

"Know you if it be day or night?" she asked Neryi.

"Dusk has fallen, and darkness will come in another hour. We know the temple, Lady, and there is food stored here for those in just such case as we. Will you join us, while night comes again into the city?"

Food . . . for a moment the thought made her reel. Not since her feast of mushrooms had she eaten.

Neryi saw that in her eyes, and the Asyi hurried to draw from hidden cupboards dusty bottles of ancient wine, sealed packets of dried fruits, stone jars of pre-served meats. Though the stuff was palatable, long storage had taken away much of the flavor, but never had Yinri tasted better fare than this. Slowly, with restraint that was as much her training with Arbold as it was the maturity of her other self, she ate. A morsel of fruit. A sip of wine. A taste of meat, a corner of journey-bread. A rest between, feeling for stomach cramps, then a bit more all round.

About her the Asyi ate sparingly, as was their invariable custom. However, they noticed all that she did, watched her reasoning and her iron control, and their internal comments flowed among them.

"She is more than the prophecies say. There is no hint of the self-will that destroyed her ancient ancestor."

"True. The world from which she strayed has schooled her well."

"And, I think, she comes of strong and noble stock. There is in her a strength and a discipline that was lacking, if we have been taught truly, in the line of the Old Kings." So spoke Neryi's thought to his siblings, as he rose to pour wine all round.

The silver cups glowed dimly in the light of the single lamp, the green gems winking secretly down their sides. The Asyi held theirs high, and Yinri, smiling, followed suit, as Neryi spoke aloud:

"You Who Pattern the Worlds, forming the histories of men and of nations, hold us in your thought. You laid our land at the Heart of the Worlds—at the heart of more worlds than one—and You gave it strong and wise rulers and sensible people. In Your unfathomable weaving, You allowed the line of the kings to diminish into degradation, the stock of the folk to grow weak and foolish and at last evil. Yet we, whom You have set as Watchers over Hasyih, have known that there would come the promised queen, who will return this land to fruitfulness.

"You have rewarded the patience of our fathers, for she has come. We must go forth now to a battle more cruel than any fought with blade and bow. Help us to stand firm in our distress. Help us to hurt those who are in our charge, that they may be healed of their folly."

The cups gleamed as they were tilted and drained. The fire of the old wine warmed the inward parts of them all, seeming to add strength to their muscles and to their wills.

They rose to their feet as one, and Neryi swung wide the door. Beyond it was a spiraling stair of wrought iron that spun away into the heights of the tower that was the Temple. Yinri went forward and began to climb, and the Asyi followed.

They emerged onto a wide parapet that circled the roof. The bulk of the Empty Tower rose darkly beside its twin, and Neryi touched the girl's sleeve and whispered, "There is your home, empty these long centuries."

"I know," she said, but her eyes were not on that dark bulk. They looked downward into the streets of the city, where torches and lanterns moved fitfully to the sound of marching. She could see, from that lofty place, the armored men moving like ants about their duties. Many toiled about the great gate of the city, which was to their right. Many more stood guard at the doors of various houses and armories.

"We cannot fight them with steel," she said, her voice low and sad. "That is the kinder way. Bodies die or they heal, and either is a clean thing . . . but we must be about our business now. How do we call to them, Neryi?"

"Easily," he said, drawing from a pouch a porcelain

placque set with faceted gems. He touched the ruby, and it blazed into life with a hum of power. He touched the emerald, and it glowed sullenly green. The topaz he did not touch, but he thumbed the sapphire, and blue light sprang up all about them, lighting the tower top with eery radiance.

"The leaders are called . . . and the commons may see us for themselves," he said.

They stood waiting, as the orderly ranks in the streets became a milling mob of men who shouted and pointed upward. They were soon joined by folk from the dwellings, and a sea of tawny faces shone up at those upon the height.

Soon came Ayilli with his fellow technicians, and the Silliyi, who were the armed muscle of that powerful guild. Upon Ayilli's face Neryi felt she could detect much alarm, though the distance was really too great for certainty.

Quickly, then, came the leaders, and Neryi pointed them out to Yinri: "That is Yinom, all in yellow velvets. He calls himself King. He is shrewd, but slothfulness has sapped his will and his powers. Behind him, there beyond the tallest guard, is Syim. From him, we judge, has come the evil taint that has overlaid our land. He was . . . warped . . . as a boy. Even in our sleep, we knew something of his character. He has made himself the hands and feet of the king."

"A pretty position from which to wield undetected power," she mused, and he looked at her with a flick of surprise. The strange mixture of mature and sophisticated judgment with the appearance of a youngling startled even him at times. For an instant he had a flash of insight into the oddity of the vision confronting those who were now staring up at him. What could they think, those spoilt and venial folk, of the wild-haired child in her tattered frock who stood beside him with the demeanor of a queen—or a goddess?

Then her hand was touching his arm. "Who is that?" she breathed, her green eyes narrowed to a shining slit.

He knew without looking that Oramphis had entered the square below. Still he glanced downward, to find the thin white face with its alien black eyes regarding him closely, glancing sidewise, now and again, to snatch a look at Yinri.

"That is the priest who has held sway in the temple. He is alien to our race and our land. The jewels hold no record of his coming. Only the fact that he rose quickly among those of the short-lived race to become the Hierophant of the Temple some seven years ago. It is in my mind that much of the venom in Syim found a ready accessory in that man whose name, even, is a thing that does not belong in the Heart of the Worlds. Oramphis—"

He was interrupted by a vicious swish, and an arrow struck deeply into the wooden door behind Yinri. There was a sigh from those gathered in the square before the temple, and the voice of the king roared out over it, "Hold, you fools! The Children of the Asyi are the guardians of the world!"

VII

Neryi stepped to the edge of the parapet. "I am glad that you, at least, remember that, Yinom, King of Hasyih. It seems that those whose duty it has been to tend the lesser affairs of the land have done ill while we slept. They have forgotten our history and our destiny. Ayilli, technician that he is, has relegated Those Who Pattern the Worlds to the realm of myth and the Queen Who Is to Come to granny tales. He, being who and what he is, may perhaps be forgiven for lack of wit, but others, higher, I think, than he, have fostered such heresy in more than the technicians.

"How long has it been, Yinom, since you entered the Temple?"

The king shifted in his velvets. "I have left such religious affairs to others, Asyi," he said. "That was not my interest. It has been long."

"I felt that you had no knowledge that abominations had taken place there," said Neryi, and the stout form of the king stiffened with the shock.

"The Dark Ways have been practiced there?" he asked in a breathless croak.

"They had filled the whole temple with the fogs of filth," Neryi answered. "The lyre in the hands of the Queen Who Has Come Again labored long and desperately to cleanse the Hall of Chanting. We of the Asyi aided, but only she might have worked that deed. Kneel to her!"

A hiss so sharp that it carried even up to the tower

top broke the silent moment that followed the command. Even as the king bent his fat knees, Oramphis was scurrying to the door of the temple, only to find it locked and guarded.

He panted out into the square again and sought to lift the king to his feet.

"None has entered there!" he cried. "They lie! You rule here, Lord King, not those come-and-go Asyi. Bend no knee to them!"

With one lazy jerk of his right arm, the king swept Oramphis's feet from under him, bringing him down onto the stony pavement in a thump of elbows and bruised bones.

"Oramphis, foreign filth, I gave you let because Syim, who has been my eyes and my mouth, vouched for you. For years you have lived among us in the wealth of wisdom that is contained in the temple. Instead of learning from the jewels that hold the records of Hasyih, instead of keeping faith with those who have used you generously, you have lapped yourself in darkness and tainted the soul of the city.

"The Children of the Asyi do not lie. Had you touched one jewel to learn of the history of this land, you would have found that fact implicit in all that you learned. The accusation that you have made proves your own guilt more accurately than anything I know. Crawl away, Oramphis. Your presence is an affront to the Queen Who Has Come Again!"

From their high place, those on the tower watched the thin and white-clad shape of the necromancer scuttle awkwardly from sight. He was hindered by the now-kneeling figures that filled the square. Only one group still stood arrogantly upright, grasping their weapons. Ayilli and his armed men quite obviously did not intend to accept the new order of things.

The technician stepped forward. "Neryi!" he called, "do you think to seize the rule of Hasyih so easily? These fools—even the king!—grovel before your outworn superstitions, but we who program the jewels have learned truths about the physical world that give the lie to your very existence. And this brat who stands beside you . . . do you truly think that we who are not old and ignorant will accept such an affront to our good sense?"

He turned his head, and the rear rank, who were archers, drew their bows, arrows nocked. When he looked upward again, Yinri had stepped to the edge of the space to stand beside Neryi. Her eyes glowed a dangerous green, and her lips were curled in an ominous smile.

Her companion felt his heart grow chill. This was the look, so he had been shown, of self-willed destructiveness that long ago had touched the faces of the old kings. When her hand touched the silver-shimmering strings of the lyre, he braced himself for horror.

A crashing chord stilled the ranks of the Silliyi. Ayilli was frozen where he stood. An eery ripple of notes began to come from the instrument . . . but her hand stilled again, as if that of another had grasped it and held.

She gasped, and Neryi looked into her face. Rapidly as flying cloud shadows, her two selves were fleeting across that pale oval. Angry imperiousness alternated with anguished humanity, as her hands clung to the greenbone frame.

Disbelief began to flicker in her eyes, as the old regal self was slowly and inexorably quelled to control. When the hands relaxed upon the lyre, it was the eyes of the girl who had come, nameless, into Hasyih that looked up into his.

The childish voice said, "She must not do cruel things! I have lived long with carelessness and thoughtlessness, and they hurt me but I endured them. When I found cruelty, I ran away. I cannot live inside myself with one who is cruel. She is within me, she is angry fit to do murder, but I have quashed her down, and she will no more use my body to work only her will."

Neryi and his kindred knelt, in their turn. "We have found a queen!" they murmured, and their faces were joyful. But the child who was now the controlling part of Yinri dropped to her knees beside them.

"Do not kneel to me!" she cried. "Stand beside me, teach me the things I must know to bring this unhappy city to order and to justice. She who is within me may not always give me her aid and her wisdom. She is powerful, but she is self-willed and fickle. Be my hands, be my conscience, Children of the Asyi!"

Though Ayilli and his men stood motionless, the king creaked to his feet; and as he stood, so did the crowd about him. They looked upward in awe as the Asyi rose, one by one, to stand, three on either side of Yinri, the Queen. The blue light shone steadily about them, and they looked down upon those below, their tawny faces a strange hue in that eery light.

Yinri laid aside the lyre. Her voice was clear and young and unafraid as she said, "I have no desire to supplant you, Yinom, King. Yours is the rule of the city and its folk. I feel you to be a good man, one to be trusted with the land if you will only exert yourself in its behalf. Mine is another task. I must bring back to health the spirits of those who have been tainted and twisted by the warped teachings of Oramphis and Syim. Go in peace and kindliness. We will be friends and coworkers, you and I."

Those in the square blinked and looked about as if they had waked from a dream or a vision. Yinom beckoned to a guard, who went at once and took Syim by the arm. His blocky face was waxen, and his tawny eyes held shock mingled with dread. As he was led away across the city toward the Tower of Justice, the king and his guard moved also, leaving the square empty, for the folk followed either the king or Syim. Only the ranks of the Silliyi stood at Ayilli's motionless back.

Looking downward, Yinri bent to lift the lyre again. Sadly, she plucked from the strings a wistful melody, full of innocence and peace. The men stirred, shook their heads, looked about in bewilderment.

"Go to them, please," the girl said to Amaryi. "Lead them to one who will care for them. Teach them again . . . for I have erased all their memories, good and ill.

Perhaps this time there will be more trust, more love, less arrogance in them." She choked silent, her eyes full of tears, as Neryi took her hand and led her from the parapet and down the dark stairs into the temple.

VIII

At last the city slept, quiet under the dark sky. No light shone from the king's house, from the empty temple, or from the tower that was the home of the Queen. Deep inside that graceful structure, in a round room that was filled with ranked and glowing jewels, a light did burn, but it was buried, windowless, in the heart of the place.

Yinri, her green eyes alert and interested, sat before a polished slab in whose grooves were set porcelain placques of coded gems. Slanting from the top of the table was a mirrorlike screen.

Neryi took one of the placques from its container and set it into a slot in the surface. "There is much that you must learn of Hasyih, Yinri. These gems contain all that is known and much that is surmised about our world and its surroundings, our people, your own ancestress. Much of what you will see is painful. Some is magnificent. Your questions will all be answered here, if you have the strength to pursue the records to their end.

"I have set aside those dealing with irrelevant things that you can investigate later. Push that placque deeply into its slot, set your eyes on the screen, and see . . ."

With impatient fingers, the girl did as she was told. Then she gasped with wonder.

As if from a point in space, she could see Hasyih, in all its green-gold-blue splendor, spinning in emptiness. Except for its sun, it seemed to be uncompanioned in spaces lit only dimly by distant suns. Yet there was a sense that this was only a seeming. With a slight whir, the picture changed, and Yinri could see that shadowy spheres winged away in a circle about the planet, each of them a different misty hue.

Neryi reached over her shoulder. Laying his finger upon a ghostly sphere the shade of dew on grass, he said, "There is Ranyi, the world from which you came. See, it impinges upon Hasyih at many points, through any one of which it is possible to move, given the key or the power. Yet if you look into the sky you will not see it, for it exists in another dimension from this.

And here is Susyi. I have stood upon its frozen surface. We have found no living thing there that might ever visit our world. Each of these shadows represents a different dimension, a different world existing in that dimension. Hasyih sits at the center of those invisible realms at the Heart of the Worlds. From it or through it alone can one go from one to another of them."

Yinri nodded, her eyes intent. "The lyre was the key?" she asked.

Neryi took up another gem and replaced the one in the slot. "This is the tale of the stringing of the lyre. Though our fathers' fathers are shown herein, the time was more than long ago. The lives of the Children of the Asyi are not as those of common men." He thrust down the plate.

Before them stood half-built walls of creamy stone. Men and women came and went about them, bringing burdens, talking and laughing with those who set them carefully into place. Neryi touched a control, and the scene moved very quickly, the walls growing as if by magic into the sturdy windbreaks and barriers they now were. Inside them dwellings and towers rose, each unique but symmetrically a part of the whole. Gardens and fountains sprang into being, and the scarlet roofs blossomed under the yellow sun.

A man came, much like Neryi, and the pace slowed to follow him into the temple. He was greeted by three others, much like himself, and Neryi murmured, "Koyil, the betrayer; Guyin, most talented of all our kind, yet also traitor; Riyin, technician; and our ancient father, Noriyi. Look, now, the Queen is coming."

From an inner door moved a woman whose beauty was surpassed by the blazing intelligence of her green eyes. She was much like Yinri, and the girl knew that she was looking at her very namesake, that one who now dwelled within her. As she watched, the queen beckoned the four men into the chamber from which she had come.

As if from a terrible distance, her voice could be heard. "The frame is ready. The greenbone came from Ranyi, after proper treatment. The passage, itself, set power into the material, for it hummed as we drilled the openings for the strings. Have you come, at last, with such strings as I desire?"

Yinri could see the lyre, its shape as familiar to her

as her own hand, standing on a workbench. She saw Noriyi nod, Guyin bring forth a packet.

"Only with the aid of Those Who Pattern the Worlds did I find what I sought," he said. "Such things are not given to unaided beings of flesh. I went into the southern forest, among the strangeness and the danger, and I was given a dream that helped me to shape your strings." He drew forth a handful of silver strands that glimmered on the very edge of vision.

The Queen took them tenderly and laid them in order upon the bench. At her nod, the men began to chant in a language Yinri could not understand. The woman's hands moved to the cadences, seeming to attach the strings by intuition, for when she was done there was no need for tuning. Its pure voice was true.

"This is the Key, Children of the Asyi. It is a weapon, too, and a terrible enigma. It was given me in a vision, and I do not understand it, even though I created it. There is something in it of powers beyond our own. Yet certain things I do know. It may not be misused. It will go away into another place, if any tries.

"Even we, who have worked together to make it, do not own it and cannot entirely control it. Any one of us who denies or betrays the truths we know can lose the power to see or to sense it. It can make easy the travel from dimension to dimension. It can destroy and it can create. We must work carefully to learn its ways, for I feel that it will hold, down the lengths of time, much power over the worlds we know. I fear it, even I. We must be cautious."

"But she did not remember her own intuition," said Neryi's voice in the girl's ear. "She lived the long span of our kind, while generations of the folk came and went, and her own abilities betrayed her. She grew impatient and demanding, then cruel. Her own sons rose up against her, though they, sadly, were too much like her to improve matters. The lyre went from Hasyih, and none knew where or how. Koyil reached out his hand for power for which he was unfit, and he and his followers were driven from life—or at least from Hasyih. Guyin went with him. Our fathers' ancestor lived out his span and joined Those Who Pattern the Worlds.

"Though I dread it, I must show you the thing the first Yinri did in the temple. It resembles the horror we found there, so it will not wholly shock you. See . . ."

Another gem went into the slot, and Yinri saw the temple. The Queen stood above a stone on which lay a child. The knife in her hand was stripping away its skin, a ribbon at a time, while darkness grew about the two of them. The shrieks of the bound child were distant prickles of sound in their ears. A huge shadow enveloped them, and the queen's triumphant chant drowned out the tortured voice.

"If her sons had not risen and slain her, we have always believed that the lyre would have been used against her. Something tells us that the darkness in the temple brought forth the lyre into your hands. Oramphis, in reviving the abominations, woke the one instrument that could topple him from power. And when it returned to

Hasyih with you, that, in turn, woke us. Strange." Neryi sighed.

"In all the eons our kind has observed, we have found, almost unvaryingly, that Those Who Pattern the Worlds have set men into circumstances ideal for their growth and development. Yet men, those of the short-lived breed and even many of those of the blood of the Asyi, turn their eyes from wonders and truths and joys and contemplate the dark and the hideous. They grasp after power over others, and the means they find to employ would dishonor the beasts of the forest.

"But Those Who Pattern the Worlds still see and know. Seldom do they interfere, yet when need is greatest, those who are needed must awaken, and that which is necessary appears. They will not guide our hands or our thought, but they have given into your keeping the lyre. That is reassurance enough to strengthen us for terrible effort."

Neryi absently arranged the placques, his eyes on Yinri. Then he held forth another. "This tells of a thing that nearly concerns us both. Hear it last, now, for you must rest."

She nodded, her dark curls moving against her cheek, and set the white shape into the slot. Long she listened, her head nodding with understanding or agreement. As the last gem winked to life, her eyes widened. She turned them upon Neryi and looked at him as if to search out his soul. When the thing darkened, she took it from the slot and laid it neatly, edge to edge with the table, but her expression was abstracted, her eyes turned inward.

The Asyi said nothing, letting her digest her new knowledge in peace. And at last she turned her head and looked at them, one by one.

So like in faces and forms, yet so different in their persons and thoughts. Neryi, square and strong, clever-handed and great of mind and heart; Amaryi, smaller, slenderer, tawny-skinned and golden-eyed and percep-tive of things unspoken and unseen; Anyi, who saw afar without effort, understanding that which others could not see; Ziniyi, holder of healing arts for mind and body; and after the three sisters the last two brothers, Lonyi, teacher to the short-lived folk; Eryi, holder of the balance, judge of final acts and thoughts. Six who were now her kindred, also.

Neryi who, by the ancient law, must be her husband. She stood and went to him as he sat on an ivory stool, waiting, his face quizzical, as it always was in time of un-certainty.

She laid her hand on his tawny club of hair, almost the same hue as his skin. "When the time has come, Neryi of the Asyi, when we know one another well, in mind and in heart, I will be happy to be your wife. For now, I am more than happy to be your kin. Is it enough for you?"

He looked into her eyes as she knelt beside him. "Which Yinri is speaking to me?" he asked. "I would not hold either half to a bargain made by those long dead."

The green eyes danced with amusement, a glint of

mischief on their surfaces, a deeper pleasure within their depths.

"Both of us," said Yinri the Queen.

IX

Autumn tinged the southern wood, touching climbing vines with scarlet and gold, drying away the ferns. Now the meadows rolled golden to the north and east, carpeting the way to the city with brittle glory. Within the city of Hasyih the parasol-shaped trees leaned their bright tops over still pools that mirrored the fleeting brilliance.

Within the Queen's Tower all was clean and still and at peace, only stirred by quiet footfalls and the hum of busy voices. The faces of the many servants were bright with new hope as they moved about the tasks of the Queen's house. Every chamber was tenanted, and teachers and scholars from end to end of Hasyih delighted in the store of knowledge preserved there and now released for the instruction of the people.

In a large chamber, lighted from above by the clear light of the mellow autumn sun, Yinri sat, with Neryi and Ziniyi beside her. With them, seated in an arc before them, were Ayilli and his men, now returned partway from the strange second childhood into which Yinri had thrust them. Their lesson was just ended, and they rose at Neryi's gesture, hurrying out with joyous haste and oddly boyish voices shouting and laughing; the combination was strange when one noted their bearded faces, marked with the lines of maturity.

Looking after them, the Queen smiled. "They are the last, my husband. In this short span of time we have worked well, healing those who were twisted by the horrors in the Temple and the false teachings of Oramphis. When those twenty men are returned to their rightful ages, this part of our task will be done."

Her face darkened as she turned her green eyes upward to meet his.

"Must you all sleep soon? We have had so little time . . ."

He touched her cheek. "We need not return to our deep rest for a very long time, Yinri. Our ancestors were not cruel, even though they wrenched their own lines of blood away from those of their own kind, who are now our short-lived cousins. With mind and will and mechanical means, they extended our spans to their present length, giving us time and opportunity to learn and assimilate many things that our cousins the Hasyisi cannot live long enough to comprehend. They were just, in their own way, and they were wise. Their wisdom dictated that your line, when embodied in a ruling king or queen, should be one with your short-lived subjects. But they knew that like attaches to like, and as long as you live, I will not be required to go into the little death that is our sleep.

"And also, there is yet danger to Hasyih. I do not know, cannot tell what it is or from whence it will come. Something dire whispers to my spirit, and the Children of the Asyi must remain awake to stand guard. The little healing that we have done here is good and healthful, but it is in my heart that the sickness went deep and woke things best left to dream away the ages."

"Thanks be that I am so young. It will give us a long while to be together," she said in her childishly impulsive way, which made him shout with laughter.

She looked at the lyre that lay before her on a low table. "How strange to know that if I had not found the key and used it, all Hasyih might have sunk into degradation. You would have slept the sleep of nightmare, and there would have been none to wake you." She shivered and reached for the instrument.

As her hand touched it, it shimmered with green light. The strings glowed fiercely silver for an instant. Then it melted from between her grasping fingers and was gone.

They gazed at the spot where it had been.

"Its work here is done, for now," she whispered, the statement half a question.

"And where did it go? And to what hand?" Neryi murmured. "Need calls the lyre in that fashion. I would give much to know whose . . . and where . . ."

Where the lyre had been, the sharp scent of willow hung in the still air. Then a breeze swirled the odor away, and the sun crawled across the table until shadow swallowed all.

The Rune
of the Weapon

I

THE WILLOWS hung still, their fronds drooping in the gasping heat of midsummer noon. The lyre was also still, its strings untouched by any breeze. In the stream the fish and the serpents sought out the cool deeps and the shadowed spots among the rushes. The air above the midstream waters rippled with heat-haze, distorting the bend of the channel and making the bushes and reeds dance beyond it.

From amid that shimmer a darker blotch detached itself. It became the shape of a man, plodding haltingly along the path whose dusts were now the consistency of talc. The sounds of his footfalls thumped down through the earth, vibrating through the water until the things that lived deep within it moved fretfully, their midday retreat disturbed.

The cool clearing beneath the hanging lyre held a flat stone that was an open invitation to rest. There the streambank curved inward, making a shallow pool that was starred with great open waterlilies. Peace lay upon the place like a great warm hand, and the traveler blinked as he came out of the last patch of sunlight and found himself possessed of a tiny plot of paradise.

With a sigh, he tugged off his incongruous woven-straw hat. Beneath it, even more incongruously, was a metal helm, whose visor had been shorn away, along with parts of its lower flange, by some brutal blow. That, too, he removed, revealing a walnut-hued face that had been tracked as much by scars as by time. Upon his lower jaw was a terrible puckered patch that corresponded well with the wound upon the helm. So eye-catching was that scar that the missing eye above it was hardly noticeable.

The other eye was gray-blue, weary, and sad. But it lighted somewhat at the sight of the inviting pool a half-pace from the stone. Seating himself, he tugged off his boots, whose soles were attached only haphazardly to their tops, and eased his hoseless feet into the still water. The tickle of a questing minnow against his toes brought a smile to his forbidding face. With that smile, the scars and wrinkles made a strange sort of accommodation and produced, together, a likable and warm expression.

There was movement about his threadbare jerkin tail, and he reached into an improvised pocket and drew forth a small furred creature that proceeded to sit upon his knee, wrinkling its leaf-shaped nose and twitching tufted ears this way and that. Gently, he set in on the path, and it scuttered to the water and drank deeply. Then it looked its companion in the eye and said, "*Chrrrrk!*"

Regretfully, the man turned another ill-sewn pouch inside out and said, "My friend, I have no crumb left. Not one. Unless you can find something hereabout to your taste, you will have to wait. Now if you were only the child, you could catch us a fish. Her sly hands were made for such work, it seemed. These stiff things have lost their cleverness.

"Still, we cannot be too far behind her now. The kitchen wench at Indris said it had only been days since she ran away." He frowned at the gently swirling water. "I have followed her for three years. Surely we are about to come close. She is growing to be a woman and will need old Arbold for protection. She is the only family I have ever had, Chirri. I am the only one left who will take care of her. We must find her!" A breeze moved down the corridor formed by the stream and its attendant forest. The lyre's strings vibrated minutely, but the man's wary ears caught the tiny hum. With one swift motion, he was on his bare feet, battered blade in hand. He scanned the path in both directions looked across the stream and into the forest behind him. There was nothing to be seen. Then, as the girl had done, he looked upward, and the strange shimmer of the greenbone caught his eye.

It hung lower than it had. Perhaps because Arbold could never have climbed after it, lamed as he now was. With his blade he hewed off the slender wand on which it hung. It fell into his waiting hand.

"A pretty toy, Chirri!" he said softly. "She would have loved such a thing. And here is a mark . . . a rune, by all the gods! Which rune, now . . . not door, no that one's a bit different. A key! A rune of a key. Just at the top. Doesn't balance. There should be more to make a proper decoration. Still, it's a gift, eh? Can't fault a gift from . . . a willow tree!"

Awkwardly, he tucked the thing into his arm, recollecting the way he had seen it done. He touched the strings with his stiff fingers. True and full, the ragged scale trilled out into the hot stillness of the day. The little beast, charmed, skittered up his knee and sat beneath the bottommost curve, feeling the vibrations of the notes from whiskers to tail.

"It's well that you're not really knowing about music," said Arbold, "or you'd bite me for making such an awful din. I like the sound, though. It's green and cool and peaceful."

They sat there in the pool of peace beneath the willow, and the battered man ran his fingers along the strings, trying, after a time, varied combinations of notes, different intervals. It seemed as if no ugly sound could come from the instrument, for, though no real music lived in his fingers, his ear was true.

Noon slipped by, and the sun moved behind the western trees. A breeze began to blow steadily, riffling the water in midstream. Still Arbold sat with Chirri on his knee . . . or his shoulder or his head . . . plucking clear notes from the silver strings. At last he sighed and drew his boots onto his sore feet.

"We'll not catch up to her thus, my chuck," he said to the little beast, tucking it into his jerkin-tail pouch with its furry head thrust out at the top. "She was here, for I can feel it. Her feet walked this path, her eyes looked upon the water. I do not question it. She is not behind us, so she must be ahead."

He lifted his small bundle to his shoulder and once again set out along the path. Where the girl had danced her lively jig, he limped to random notes, and the sun slid down behind the forest.

At the point where Yinri had found her door's entryway, Arbold paused to favor his painful leg. The path behind had become a tunnel of deep shadow, and the stream had changed from green-gold laughter to blue-purple purring. Night was no more than a half-step over the horizon, and Arbold knew that his weary limbs could go little further. Looking about for shelter, he saw the selfsame berry thicket that had led the girl into Hasyih. For him it held no door into otherwhere, but the thickly twining vines and branches offered protection from the dews that tormented his bones with their chill dampness.

Though he had nothing with which to stay his own hunger, he knew that the tiny beast in his pocket was ravenous. Crawling into the nook, he sat heavily and painfully and drew the creature forth once again. A twig broken from the bushes provided a digging tool, and he proceeded to excavate for bugs and worms. There in the cool and loamy spot they abounded, and he presented a pale beetle to Chirri, who regarded it with resignation, if not enthusiasm, and began to nibble at its bulbous rear.

Then Arbold unrolled his bundle and spread the scrap of wool in which it had been wrapped. It was the other half of the blanket that Yinri had used, a bit insufficient for his greater length and girth but better than the cool earth under him. As darkness wrapped him round, the old soldier dozed in his skimpy covering,

Chirri tucked snugly into the curve of his neck that was sheltered by his short beard.

The door into Hasyih did not open. That way was not for him. Instead, far upstream, a boat tugged gently at its tethering rope and ring. A weir that abutted the stone wall to which it was tied loosed a bubbling froth of water, as its shuts were opened. The swirling current danced beneath the boat, all but drowning the inaudible last echoes of lyre notes. With a whisper of hemp, the knot slid apart, and the craft slipped away from its mooring into the stream and ghosted down the dark waters, answering the call of the lyre.

Ranyi, the moonless world, turned in its sleep beneath the teeming stars. Dawn slid up the east, and the first hint of light brought Arbold to wakefulness. Groaning almost silently, he worked his stiff limbs, stretched his fingers until they were again capable of grasping and holding. By the time the light was glimmering on the water, he had his pack rolled, his blade fixed to his belt, and was ready to go on his way upstream.

Yet some instinct held him still for a short time. He knew that his child had been in this spot. The cord of attachment and affection strung between them had led him here. Now it seemed to hang slack. No tug drew him upstream, though he knew that his direction must lie there. As a dog snuffles in circles about the spot where he lost a trail, so Arbold moved about uneasily, casting a short way upstream, then returning to the original spot.

Dawnlight was streaking the gray waters with silver

when a dark shape slipped into view from the midst of a screen of willow fronds. Arbold, troubled and pacing, glanced at the stream as the boat slid into the eddy that curled toward shore. He stood as if frozen and watched the dark-painted craft ease itself onto the sliver of sand at the bank.

Chirri, again in his pocket pouch, chittered excitedly as the man moved forward to bend and catch the trailing rope. Arbold drew the boat safely onto the shelving verge and stood looking at it. In the middle of the narrow hull was a bag that sagged heavily against the plank seat spanning its midsection. Moving carefully, the man stepped in and pulled the bag toward him. Its top was secured with a twist of string, which he loosed. It was filled with freshly milled flour.

The old soldier gave a subdued whoop. "Chirri, my chuck, we'll have breakfast!" he said. And in a very few minutes he had a panikin from his pack filled with a sticky mix of flour and water, flavored with a pinch of salt from his saltbox. A fire was the work of moments, and his little skillet soon sat over red coals with a flour cake browning within it.

Though his old inwards were used to long fasts, Arbold felt inordinately cheered and encouraged when they were securely chinked with the cakes. Chirri, too, had had his fill of crumbs and was *chrrrking* softly. They sat together on the aftermost seat of the boat, watching the now thinly gilded wavelets break at its prow.

"Now we must decide what to do," the old warrior

murmured to his companion. "We should go on up the stream. That is the direction she took. And yet I can't feel that she's there. I'm getting old, Chirri. I wasn't notional when I was younger. The child was here, but she isn't now. My legs are getting worse by the day, and they'll carry me precious little onward. Here at our feet is a neat little craft, dry and tight, all stocked with flour. It's a fool's choice, after following a trail for three years, but I will go down, Chirri, my chuck, in the green boat on this green stream. Perhaps the gods have heard me, at last. Or perhaps I am too old and useless to be of any help to my child, even if I should find her. What do you think?"

"*Chirrirrirk!*" said the little animal emphatically.

"Exactly," said Arbold, dipping the hissing-hot skillet into the stream, then scouring it with a handful of willow twigs. He scuffed out the remains of the fire, tidied his pack and stowed it away in the bow of the boat, then turned to look at the area once again. In the light of the rising sun, it was a serene spot, and he felt more strongly than ever that the child had stood there before going—where?

"Not upstream!" he said aloud and turned to seat himself carefully in the little boat. He felt about beneath the seats for some sort of oar, but all he found was a stout walking stick and a packet of resin for patching holes in boat hulls. Further rummaging into nooks and crannies under the planking that made a walkway over the ribs of the bottom brought forth a stout line and a tangled mess of fishhooks.

His tracked face broke into a smile. "Aha, Chirri, we'll have fish for our supper, wait and see. And even flour to dredge it in. The gods who attend to our sort have provided well for us, eh?"

The creature didn't answer, being engaged in what looked to be a game that involved noticing every ripple that washed past their bow. Arbold, having no way either to propel or to steer his new transportation, stretched his legs along the planking and leaned his back against the edge of the seat behind him. The willows moved past above him in dreamy silence, and the *lap-lap* of the little waves was hypnotic. Warmed by the sunlight he drifted into far deeper sleep than he had known in many nights.

II

The stream was a lazy one, lying between low forests and fields on either side. It looped gently to and fro, untroubled by rapids or extreme shallows or sandbanks, and the dark green boat glided smoothly down the current. After a time, when the sun had ridden up the sky almost to noon, it entered a long stretch of dark water that was shadowed by great oak trees. When the boat passed into this tunneled way, Arbold woke and sat to see his surroundings.

All about him stretched wide reaches of forest, tenanted by trees so old that no younger and smaller growth could be seen to clutter the even mold of the floor. The sun was a mere confetti of twinkles above the arching branches. The soldier shivered, for the quiet of the place was not that of a forest at noon. It hinted at old secrets that he wished to avoid knowing.

The stream's windings had been eased almost to straightness, and he began to look closely at the banks that held it to so strange a course. In time, he found a spot where the tangle of reeds was thin, and he could see that, as he had thought, the verges were made of cut stones. He knew that at the point where he had boarded the boat the stream had been completely natural; but that was now far behind him, and he knew he had found another sort of place entirely.

Once he saw steps, all but hidden in a tangle of creepers. They led down to the water beside a protruding stone that he knew must have rings set into it for the tethering of boats. Again, dark in the dim distances of the wood, he saw a bulk whose clean outlines had been shattered at one side, and he knew it as a hold of the Ancient Days, for that style of uncluttered and undefended building had long been lost.

Thoughtfully, he loosened his old blade and laid it across his lap. He had never tried it against ghosts of the past, but it was better than no weapon at all. Then he thought of the lyre, which he had put on the middle seat of the boat. Making a long arm, he reached it forth and tucked it into his arm. Chirri, silent and watchful in the bow, scurried to sit between his thighs, twitching his whiskers in anticipation.

"Better to make music than to sit and dread the silence, eh, Chirri?" the man asked, running his thumbnail across the strings. A silver ripple of sound followed it up the scale, and the forest all about seemed almost to reel in shock. The silence became painful to the ear, but Arbold, with a chuckle that he didn't truly feel, picked out a simple rhythm on three notes of the lyre, and its greenbone frame seemed to glow with quiet amusement.

They slid quietly down the stream that was now a small river, and the lyre was busy all the way. Improving a bit with practice, he attempted a jig, with Chirri's uncritical approval. Tiring of that, he lay back, Chirri on his chest, and struck random notes that purled away through the wood, ripping its strange silence with their defiance.

The afternoon wore away, and at last the trees began to thin a bit. They were as large, but their ranks grew less, leaving glades that caught the slanting light from the west and channeled it toward the stream. In the grip of the river, the boat now hurried down its way, and Arbold, feeling the nearing of something strange and final, tucked Chirri into his pouch, slipped his pack onto his shoulders, his blade into its worn sheath, and took the lyre on his lap.

Ahead, he began to see a bright patch that must be the end of the wood. The stone banks grew higher, broken often by steps and odd bulwarks of white stone that seemed to have been poured, so seamless was its texture. A round building, low and featureless, slid past. Its bubblelike shape was amazingly regular to one accustomed to seeing only rough-hewn stone laid by laboring muscles. The slanting sunlight washed it finely in pale gold, and no shadow marked a join.

Its top was a jagged ruin, shattered outward from within, it seemed to Arbold's knowing eye. Bits of the masonry lay scattered about it, half-hidden in weeds and brush patches, and they, too, were as regular and flawless as pieces of eggshell.

Now the soldier sat on the seat, scanning the shoreline closely. There were more structures, now, low domes and irregular arcs of the pale stuff, lying as if puddled in random trenches and hollows. Ahead, a larger mass caught the light, and its shape was marvelous to behold.

A tower, phallic in shape, smooth and featureless, rose from what appeared to be concentric circles of molded masonry, each a half-story lower than the one before; thus the tower thrust upward from a mounded warren with the dimensions of a town. This had not been a keep, as the lords of the land now knew them.

His blade was now in his hand. The sun, almost set, tenanted the place with shadows, and his instinct told him that any danger here would be such as he had never encountered. But all was lifeless as the boat slipped along beside the low curbing that edged the water and nosed into a curve beside a rusted ring.

"Well, Chirri, it looks as if the boat, at least, has come home," he murmured, but only a very muffled "*Chrrrk!*" answered him.

He might have pushed the craft away from the curving dock, sent it on down the river. That was not Arbold's way. The impulsiveness that had moved him to pluck the child from the melee in her father's keep also moved him to set his foot on the stony verge and to tie the boat securely to that convenient ring.

Now the sky blazed with sunset color, but the sun itself was down. The top of the tower glowed crimson, though its base sat in purple shadow. Taking his bearings as well as he could in so alien a place, he made for the arch of a gate that led from the streamside into the body of the keep-city. Inside, night had all but come to the broad and regular curves of the streets he found there.

Exactly similar doorways curved darkly in the seamless walls on either hand. No shelter, he felt, could be found in these lower ways. The tower was different. His instinct drew him toward it, the magnet of its mystery drawing the steel of his curiosity inexorably.

He found with some astonishment that his left hand still held the lyre, his right being occupied with his worn sword. Wary, now, of making any unnecessary sound, he made as if to lay it against a handy wall, but the instrument glowed up at him, green and silver, and his hand would not leave it there.

Bent there in the dark street, he felt a presence. He looked up, then straightened in surprise; his hand loosed the blade it held, though the other held fast to the lyre.

A woman stood before him, and in her hand she held what was a weapon, though it was unlike any ever used in any time or place he had known. It glittered ice-blue and searing white, its cold gleam shining even through the pale flesh of her hand, making the veins show as rosy lines and the bones as dark ones. Yet, though the hand was frail to the point of transparency, its grip on the weapon was sure. The weapon held all the power that its holder lacked, for a slender beam, like flame, licked from its conelike point.

She was tall, that woman, and her hair was pale as the flame in her hand. She was gaunt with illness or hunger, and her eyes were over-large, glittering eerily in the dark pits of their sockets. Her scanty smock was white, giving her whole figure a ghostlike distinctness.

Arbold straightened slowly, taking care to make no threatening move. The lyre settled into the proper position, as if by itself, so that when he faced the woman his hands were in place for playing. Disturbed by the motion, the place, or his own instincts, Chirri thrust his head from the pouch and *chrrked* loudly.

The woman jerked, her hand tightening on the unearthly weapon, and its beam lengthened and swept erratically toward Arbold. Faster than thought or reflex could explain, his hand crashed down on the strings, sending wild notes into the air before him. As the beam intersected their trajectories, each note seemed to lick into flame . . . but the beam did not penetrate their shield.

The street was silent for long moments before the woman said, "Who are you? None come here except those who roam the wood. They are rough and cruel, and they have no defense against my weapon. You . . . are different."

"Yes," Arbold answered simply. "I have been brought here, I think, by powers that you and I do not know. This lyre, it comes to me now, summoned the craft that brought me here. It stopped that dire thing you hold from—what? Burning me to ashes? Worse, I suspect. It holds potencies that I cannot predict.

"Yet now we are here, wherever here is, what do we do now? I need shelter for the night, though I have flour in the boat."

"You have food?" she whispered, and her hand loosed its grip of her weapon until its fires were cooled to darkness. "All is gone. Every one of the sealed containers that we found in the city has been used or is spoiled. Urthant is dead of fever that would not have killed a well-nourished man. And I have waited here for death—or for those marauders from the forest to find me when I grow too weak to lift the weapon."

Arbold grunted. "Have you fire?" he asked. "I can retrieve the bag from the boat, if you will make enough light with that strange thing so that I make no false turning in the darkness. Then we can make flour cakes, which are not relished by the great and powerful, but which are mightily filling to the belly. If, of course, you can make fire."

"That I can do," she said, grasping the thing with renewed energy until its chill glow danced through the street ahead of them.

She led him, burdened eventually with the bag, through the streets, up invisible corridors that echoed hollowly to their steps, past doors that creaked wearily open and croaked rustily shut. And at the end of the blind and trusting journey, he found himself in a great

round room whose white and windowless walls shone
in the most unnatural light that the soldier had ever seen.

He could see no torch, no lamp, no cunning arrangement of wires and glass manned by a panting servitor
such as he had seen, once or twice, in keeps whose lords
dabbled in the old ways. It seemed that the stone itself
must emit the white radiance, or that it was shed from
the entire expanse of the high ceiling.

His hostess gave him no time to gape. She went to a
white slab set at the side of the chamber and drew from
a cupboard a squat device, also white, that she attached
by a cord to a slot in the wall. Its flat surface didn't
change, but when she touched a damp finger to it it
sizzled with heat. He lost no time in mixing his cakes
and dropping one onto that weird cooking-machine.

It smelled entirely satisfactory, and he took it up with
his belt knife and offered it to the woman, who received
it on a plate of homely crockery and proceeded to de-
vour it, while he dropped more batter to cook. It took a
number of makings to satisfy both, and Chirri ate one
entire cake with gusto. But when all were filled to
capacity, there still remained questionings.

After Arbold had recounted the circumstances that
had brought him to this strange city, the woman looked
long at him, as if to ferret out his inner workings. Then
she nodded slowly, as if making a decision.

"I have pretended," she said, "that Urthant and I
were rightful tenants of this place, heir to the powers
that are still left here. We came by accident—or else we

were guided here, all unknowing. War destroyed our farm and all the villages nearby. Even the fields were burned and sowed with salt in the bitterness of that conflict. Our neighbors sat and wailed and starved amid the ruin. We were another matter.

"I see that I must tell you a bit of older history. Urthant was the younger son of Olwan, who was lord of a small holding far to the west of this place. I was Enid, oldest child and heir of Arennath, and he was the richest and most powerful lord thereabout. When Urthant came courting me, I received him willingly, thus angering my father to black rage. I was no chattel nor dupe, and so I told my folk. If following my own inclination meant giving up my heritage, then so be it. And so it was."

Here Arbold chuckled. The food, the excitement of company and conversation had smoothed away the gaunt look of the woman, and he could see a trace of her young beauty returning to her now-flushed cheek. More than a trace of the will and determination that had brought her through her tumultuous life were apparent in her bearing.

She looked at him sharply, then went on. "Olwan had no desire to cut himself off from the largesse my father granted to those about him, so he, too, disowned his child, and we two went away to the east carrying nothing but our hands and our heads and the little that we owned. Among the things that were truly ours was a bit of land that Urthant's grandmother had given him when he was born. To that wild spot we went, camping like brigands in the wood until we were able to clear fields and to build a house with the trees thus felled.

"We were young and strong and filled with anger, so our toil went like the wind. In five years we had achieved a farm and a home and two children. Neighbors crept into the lands about us, over the years, and we grew older and less energetic. Still, our younglings were growing tall and strong, and neighbor aided neighbor, when there was need. We looked likely to sink comfortably into age and to go quietly to our graves, in time.

"But there came war. We had—and still have—no inkling of its causes or even of its participants. Armed men swarmed the countryside like ants, and where they went nothing remained. Our stout house vanished in smoke and flame, and our two sons were slain defending it. We came in time, their father and I, to see the roof fall. We found their bones in the warm ashes.

"We would not sit keening into the wind, as the others did. We set out, once again, with only ourselves . . . but our tally was lessened, for we no longer had either youth or hope. Only our tough refusal to bend our necks to the will of chance sent us eastward. We crossed the river to the south, where skeletons of fantastic bridges still span its breadth.

"We turned north simply because in that direction there was a path that beasts had worn into the forest on their way to water. We walked and dug roots and caught incautious hares in snares and learned to tickle fish from the river pools. And we came here, where no foot had entered for years uncountable."

Arbold grunted with comprehension. Then he asked, "What of the brigands in the wood? Were they here then, or did they come later, displaced by the warring?"

"We were fortunate, at first. No two-legged being roamed these strange lands then. The city stood untouched save only by time and the workings of the land and the beasts and birds. Its storage rooms were stocked with unfamiliar foodstuffs, sealed tightly into metal so that one must hack the containers open with a stout blade. Still, many of them held fruits and vegetables that were still tasty and nourishing.

"Strangest of all, we found that a power still lived here, as it does to this day. Light appears here in the tower whenever you enter a room and is quenched when you leave it. Down in the lower depths there are chests filled with cold more intense than that of winter. In those there is meat, but how could it still be healthful after so very long? We could not bring ourselves to venture to use it. Even when we began to starve, we were warned by something inside us not to try that source of food."

"So you found that weapon here and learned to use it?" queried the soldier, his interest focused on the untoward thing.

"There are several such in a room just above this. We went very cautiously, you may be sure, in our testing of them. Some would come to life for Urthant and not for me. Others were in the reverse. But they saved us when the wild men began to steal into the city from the forest, seeking food and shelter.

"Make no mistake . . . they could have had both, and welcome. But they were returned to the animal. They tried to kill my man and to ravish me, when we were showing them about the place. Only the fact that they did not recognize this as a weapon saved us. You are right, it does things far worse than burning to human flesh."

She shuddered and fell silent, and Chirri scurried from his spot between Arbold's feet and flowed up her knee. He sat there chirruping softly, and she smiled and ran a finger about his ear, sending him into a quiver of ecstasy. Then, taking up the little animal, she said to Arbold, "You are weary, I have no doubt. We made our sleeping places in the building that joins this, for we have not found the secret of quenching these lights for sleep. There are pads and fabrics of unknown fibers here, and we made ourselves very comfortable."

They moved from the round room, and as Arbold moved through the doorway the lights dimmed slowly. When the door whispered shut, it was upon darkness. A corridor circumscribed the tower, its doors opening outward into the abutting building and inward, one in each quadrant, into that chamber they had left. Enid led the way, now using her weapon again for light, to one of the doors and set the heel of her hand against a panel beside it.

The door slid into the thickness of the wall, and the two entered. There was a soft click, and a round globe in the center of the ceiling popped into brightness. On intricately fretted silver frames lay pads of bright fabric. With a nod, Enid passed into an adjoining room, leaving her bewildered guest to his rest.

III

Arbold woke to total darkness. Only the limp warmth of Chirri, asleep as usual beneath his beard, was familiar. For a moment he lay disoriented, listening, feeling, smelling the air about him. There was the limey, dusty, infinitely *old* smell of the white stone. There was a faint bittersweet scent that was Enid's. There was the bark-fresh-air-leaf smell of Chirri. There was, very faintly, the thrum of some deep-seated vibration, so indigenous to the place that he had not noticed it until most of his senses were foreclosed to him.

He tried to remember the direction in which lay the button that Enid had touched to produce light, and to quench it again, but he was in that detached just-after-sleep state in which nothing comes clear. At last he sat, waking Chirri, who *chirrked* irritably, and rose to shuffle cautiously toward the spot where he thought the door to Enid's room might be.

The room had been bare, except for the couch and a chair and desk against the wall farthest from the door, so he moved without impediment. Fetching up against the wall, he felt carefully along it until he found the gap that was the doorway.

"Enid?" he called softly. "Are you awake?"

There was no answer, no sound of breathing, and

he knew that she had risen and was already about whatever her business might be in this eery pile of masonry. He went on following the wall on the other side of the space, setting his seeking hand, at last, on the outer door. As he fumbled for the plate that opened it, it whisked into the wall and let in a flood of light that set him blinking madly. Enid was nearby.

"I have made cakes," she said. "And you might like to bathe, later," which he took to be a delicate hint that he was less than aromatic, after his rough span of journeying.

Leaving his tattered boots, he went barefoot over the cool stone, finding that she had activated lights that now set the corridor ablaze. The round room welcomed them with brightness again, and he perched on a tall stool at the high slab and matched Enid's appetite, cake for cake.

When all the cakes were reduced to crumbs, which Chirri could not attempt to clear away, so distended was he with his own breakfast, Arbold asked, "What was this room, do you suppose? Did you ever find a clue as to its uses?"

"It was a working-place," she said. "Look," and she touched a switch on the wall before her. Above them, the smooth wall cracked open to reveal shelving lined with strange utensils of glass and metal. There were racks of short, round-bottomed tubes that might have admitted a man's finger. There were metal frames holding beautifully shaped flasks with cone-shaped bottoms. There were small dishes of odd shapes, large pitcherlike vessels of glass, in truth oddments of a multitude of incomprehensible varieties and uses.

"They used this somewhat as a woman uses a kitchen or a physician uses his compounding-room," said the woman. "But there is no way in which we can know what their purposes were, for the books that survive in lower cabinets are in a lettering unlike any I have ever seen. And even those have been eaten by insects and are fragile as lace. We were not unlettered, Urthant and I, and we passed many a day in seeking to unravel their secrets. Perhaps you might look at them, if you have knowledge of any scripts other than those in use in this continent."

"I am no scholar," he said, "but I have rummaged into strange places and set eyes on odd manuscripts, from time to time. Still, my business has been war, and only the maimings of my last battle have turned me aside from it. A one-eyed man has many vulnerable areas, when it comes to combat. Once I thought of laying aside my blade—but the child needed things that I thought to give her by just a short time more of mercenary service."

"You, too, had a child . . . and lost it?" asked Enid.

"Not my own blood," he answered, "yet as close, mayhap, as if she had been. I plucked her from a burning keep and set her behind me. Those green eyes stared up from the terror of trampling hooves so pleadingly, but so bravely, that I could not leave her there. For seven years she went with me, camping in forests and moors, hiding in safe nooks while I was about my business, learning all the inappropriate things that one of my calling and experience could teach her. Few gentle arts were among them, I fear, but I did teach her that of reading. She was apt. If fate had used her justly, she would have been the adornment of some keep or a House of Philosophy."

"And you have been searching for her . . . how long?" asked the woman.

"For over two years," he said. "I was a long time mending, after that raid that ended my fighting days. She had thought me dead, along with those I rode with. My band, I think, had envied me her company and promised me that should I fall they would see that she found a place to live. So they took her away and left her at the first house with a woman to care for her. That place was swept by plague that took most of its inhabitants.

"In some way, her life has been charmed. Whatever dire thing has happened to those about her, she has survived to go forward. I have traced her through six stopping-places. Most of them, I suspect, she left in anger and haste. The last of them she fled to escape its master, who intended to make her his leman. She went away up this very stream, for I followed her to a spot beyond which my heart told me that she had not gone. Yet she was not there. Strange. But along that path I found this lyre, and it is no common thing. It was sent, I think, to lead me to her at last."

"It seems to be a potent thing," said Enid. "Nothing has ever withstood the fire-blade that I carried last night. Those from the forest have come bringing talismans of many different sorts, blessed—or cursed—no doubt by whatever they call a holy man. And that gives me a thought.

"Below us, in the chambers where the chests of frozen meats are, there is a door. Only once did Urthant and I open it, and it was difficult, indeed. Then we were sorry that we had made the effort. There is a chamber there that holds frozen men and women. We were terrified, and we closed the door behind us when Urthant said that he saw one of them move, very slightly. Now the door will not open again."

Arbold grunted. "And you, being the woman you are, want to take another look, just to be certain. However, I am in no hurry. I will be led, I do not doubt, in the direction I must go. Until such time, I am at your disposal. Let me only find something with which to cover my feet. Bad as my boots were, their soles did dissipate the chill of stone."

"That is easily remedied," said Enid. "This was a place stocked with all that its people needed. When the inhabitants left, whatever sent them forth, they did not disturb the caches. There is a room full of footwear. Come."

They went about the curving hall to another door, which opened to Enid's hand. She activated the light, and Arbold looked about in astonishment. The walls were lined with cases that were faced with glass of such fineness that even with eons of dust upon them their contents were not obscured.

He wandered along before the displayed shoes and boots, searching for something that looked as if it might be kind to his scarred feet. When he saw a low boot with a thick, soft-looking sole, he pointed to it and said, "That one, I think."

Enid slid her finger down a row of perforations at the joining of the nearest panes, and the glass slipped aside. Reaching inside, the soldier found that the boots were sealed inside a tough but invisible layer of something. It resisted his efforts at tearing it, and Enid took up the parcel and worked her fingers along the seam at the top. In a moment, there was a sigh of air rushing out of—or into?—the package, and the boots were in his hand. They might have been made and put there yesterday.

He set his sore feet into them, and they nestled into the greatest comfort he could recall in years. No seam pinched or rubbed, no tightness evinced itself. The things seemed to adapt themselves to him with the deftness of a good servant. He sighed with pleasure.

"Not since I left my father's house have I had a truly good pair of boots," he said. "Almost the thought of that single thing sent me home again, more than once. Yet, though I could get along well with my father's bootmaker, I could not abide my father. For the first time since I was seventeen, my feet are at ease."

Enid chuckled and rose from the stool she had perched upon. "Come, now, and we will see if that stubborn door will open to the notes of your lyre," she said, and he followed her from the room.

Though they passed a ramp that flowed downward into darkness from the level of the corridor, the woman

gnored it. Instead, she touched a button that slid open a
door that led into a small blind box of a room, hardly
larger than would accommodate the two of them.

"This is a conveyance," she said to Arbold, who
started as the door whispered shut, sealing them into
that small, ill-lit space.

He nodded, but every instinct cried out, "Danger!"
as the thing fell away beneath his feet. Nothing untoward happened, however, as it moved silently downward.

It stopped, and the door opened of itself. Blackness
filled the space outside the door, but Enid ran her hand
along the wall of the new corridor and touched something that activated a long row of flat plates, which
glowed with a cold hue. Then she fastened the door of
the conveyance open with a bit of wire and a hook that
had obviously been rigged by Urthant or herself.

"This way," she said, turning right. They went
twenty paces, then she opened a very wide door, ample
in size to admit six men on horseback. The halves swung
inward, instead of sliding into the walls. The room began
to glow, reluctantly, it seemed to Arbold, into life.

Its shape was square. He decided that it was far beneath the soil-level, unconstrained by the tower-shape
as was the room above. Its walls were lined with white
chests large enough to contain a half-dozen men. Enid
lifted the lid of one, and he could see, through a light
film of frost crystals, the shapes of joints and ribs that
filled it. He agreed, silently, that such fare was best left
alone.

Now Enid moved across the deep chamber to a narrow door that was set, like a sally port, in a larger opening that could be opened at need to admit something very large, indeed. There was no button or latch that he could see.

"Urthant touched it with one of the fireblades, and it opened, but it would never open again to that touch," she said. "That is why I thought your instrument might have a power capable of opening the door once more. I have been uneasy, here alone, at the thought of those beings—dead or not—beneath my feet in their cold chamber."

"Power makes life," Arbold mused, setting the lyre into his arm. "Could it be that this whole tower came to life at your urgings, and in so coming . . . perhaps brought something . . . someone . . . out of long sleep?" He touched the strings, running his finger gently from front to back. The ripple of sound seemed to eddy about them, each note holding its place in harmony with its companions. The lights flared brighter, as if new power flowed into them, and Enid's eyes widened.

Arbold shivered with sudden foreboding. His hand stilled on the strings. "It is better not!" he said sharply. "I feel danger in this. Let the door remain sealed!"

"Too late!" Enid whispered. "Some power moved!"

The door groaned as if in human agony. It began to move, swinging slowly inward. With dread, yet drawn by the motion, the two stepped into the room beyond. It was filled with blue light that made deathlike masks of their staring faces.

In the center of the square chamber stood tall crystal tubes, half again the height of a man and twice the girth of one. They were filled with something colder even than the chests outside. Scarves of vapor wafted away from their surfaces as the cold air from the outer room touched them. Yet there was no frost. The contents were quite visible.

Each of them held a human figure, glistening, frozen into stasis.

Enid's breath went out of her with a sound, "Unh!" as if she had been struck in the solar plexus. "They are not the same!" she hissed, reaching for Arbold's hand. "At least, the first one isn't! Look at him. His hand is level with his waist, as if he were lifting it. When we first saw him, both his arms hung straight down."

Arbold looked into those chill, open eyes that seemed to be looking into his very heart. The deep throb that permeated the tower seemed fractionally stronger. The lights were ghastly blue, and the old soldier felt that something long and slow and frightening had been happening in those tubes, since the day that Enid and her man brought the tower back to life.

"Where is the source of the power?" he whispered to Enid. "Did you and Urthant seek out its heart?"

"Deep under here, beneath hundreds of spans of soil, there is a sealed place of thick gray metal. In a circle about it, in a wide corridor that is more like a room with a hole in its midst, are great machines that begin to pulse when lights are lit or cookery is done. Sometimes they work when neither is being used, so we assumed they also control these rooms of cold.

"That central part is sealed away so completely that no one, I think, could find a way to enter it without knowing the secrets of its builders. There are symbols cut into its walls, all about it. A death's head glowers from its every face."

"A good place to avoid," mused the soldier, watching the forms in the tubes, wreathed, now, in floating veils of mist.

"Enid, have you ever seen any folk like to those?" he asked suddenly. "Our people are a mingled lot, dark and fair, pale-skinned and swarthy, with eyes that range from palest gray to utter black. But those . . . those are different. They are golden-eyed, and their skin is a tawny-gold. None such are in the old tales, any that I ever heard."

She looked closely, though she moved no nearer. Then she nodded. "There are tales in the west," she said. "They speak of the Yashi, who were akin to the gods themselves and who wielded power that they could not, in the end, control. I have thought, now and again, that this must be almost the last surviving hold of the Yashi, but I did not dream that they still waited here in their flesh."

IV

They did not linger long in that eery spot. The lyre refused to seal the doorway, try what tunes they would, so they had to be satisfied with pulling it shut as tightly as they could manage. Then they hurried, with one accord, to the conveyance and were lifted again to the level of the world they knew. Though they said nothing, each knew that the other was profoundly shaken. Those eyes had been knowing. They had not been dead eyes, not though they may have stared into darkness for a thousand years.

When they stood again in the corridor about the tower, they sighed with relief and moved toward the workroom to take counsel. Before they had moved three paces, they stopped to listen.

Someone was shouting within the very tower.

The voices echoed strangely through the place, and they could not fix the direction immediately. Enid led the way to the workroom in a rush, and once there she opened another cabinet and took from it a weapon much like that she had held before. This one was longer, its conelike nozzle more blunt. When she grasped it, a tongue of flame so white that it seemed to darken the bright lights of the room jetted forth.

"Will you try to find one that will work for you?" she asked Arbold.

He shook his head, his single eye bright and alert. "I have a strange feeling—an intuition, if you like—that neither blade nor blaze is needed here. The lyre, aside from acting as a key, is a weapon. My hands tell me it is, for they know weapons by the feel. My heart tells me it is, overruling my stubborn old head. I will go forth armed with the lyre, and if I fall you will still have your cold flame to protect you."

"They have never come into the city by day," Enid said sharply. "Some mischief is being tried, something new and dangerous. They feel confident, for more than one of their fellows has watched his own flesh melt and his bones crumble in the breath of this foul thing. They *fear* me. What has given them the courage to face me now?"

Arbold looked at her, eye to eye. "The lyre is here, now. In my dotage, I am coming full circle to that unshakable trust in the gods that I was taught in my cradle. They are drawn, I believe, to their own fate, whatever it must be. As we are, Lady. As the child must have been. Whether we are to die here or to live I cannot know. I simply guess that a pattern is being shaped, and we are a part of it. Come. Let's go to meet them."

She opened her mouth, but the look upon his scarred and humorous face stopped her words. She took up the weapon and followed him from the chamber, and the door hissed to behind her.

The voices now rang through the corridor, bouncing from surfaces and booming hollowly. Arbold, led by something he did not recognize, ran widdershins around the curving way, the lyre firmly held in his arm. The corridor, unlike the chamber they had left, did not light itself automatically to aid those who walked it. They ran in darkness, only the wicked glimmer of Enid's weapon lighting that black journey.

When they had reached the spot where the next of the four chamber doors opened into the hallway, Arbold stopped and motioned to Enid to do the same. Luckily, she saw his hand move by the firefly glow from the weapon and was able to halt before caroming into him.

The soldier braced his feet and his shoulders grew tense, straining with the force of something that was moving through him. Then his hand moved, the stiff fingers touching the strings of the lyre with mastery not their own. A trio of notes quested into the darkness.

Arbold gasped. The notes glowed, silvery-bright against the gloom, as they winged away down the corridor.

For a moment there was complete stillness. The voices hushed as if the throats that uttered them had been suddenly sealed. Those notes asked, more compellingly than words, "What do you do here, where you do not belong?"

The silence was broken by one single voice. It was deep and commanding, used to obedience, Arbold knew from experience. Though its words were distorted by the booming echoes, he felt that it must be exhorting men to go forward.

They came, though not willingly. He heard the clump of heavy boots, the scuff of skin-shod feet, the patter of sandals. His hand moved again, and notes flew up to hang like a galaxy of stars above the scene. When the taggled group of men rushed into view their torches were dimmed by the glow overhead, and they stopped short to stare upward.

A thin figure stepped forward, the pale narrow face even paler in the white-silver light. "They are only two!" it cried. "Kill them! Oramphis, who has traveled between the worlds, commands you to do this!"

Enid raised her weapon and tightened her grip. The terrible cone flared to brilliancy, and the men quailed. Oramphis, black eyes sparking rage, shouted again, "Kill them!"

There was hesitation among them. Then, driven by some obscure compulsion wielded by Oramphis, they moved forward again. Arbold stood in the center of the way, armed only with the lyre. They paid him no heed at all, concentrating their attention upon Enid.

Then Oramphis saw the lyre. His breath sucked between his teeth in a hiss as he drew near to the lamed soldier.

Arbold's hand fell again upon the strings. The men in the corridor fell as if boneless in a ragged windrow of sleep. Only Oramphis stood upon his feet. Silver notes swarmed about his head like disturbed bees.

The mechanisms deep inside the building surged with augmented power. Enid and Arbold could feel their throbbing even through the stone paving. As if enspelled, the three stood in the corridor, still as death, while powers none of them understood or could control woke to full potency.

Another burst of music followed Arbold's hand. These notes quivered in the air between the two and Oramphis, forming an arched opening. Under the compulsion that gripped him, Arbold caught Enid's hand and ran for that space.

They dived through into nothingness.

V

They fell, together, into a garden so steeped in sunlight and peace that the embattled place they had left seemed to have been a part of some evil dream. They lay for a while on the clipped grass, gasping with the stress of that short confrontation. The arch through which they had come still glimmered faintly in the air near the low stone wall that bordered the place, and Arbold looked at it uneasily. He little desired to bring with him that horde of vermin into this quiet spot.

The lyre lay near his hand, and he sat slowly and caught it to him. No magic lay in his fingers now, but he painfully plucked a little melody from the instrument. The arch winked out like a blown candle, and Enid smiled at him from her place under the hem of a trailing willow.

"They cannot follow us here," she said. "Wherever this is, even if its folk put us to death without cause or hindrance, it is better than what lay in that tower. Below us, while you played and the power beat through the stone, I felt those frozen . . . things . . . waking. That tower was *theirs*. Those weapons were their own, with what others that we never recognized as such? Our world lies at their mercy, Arbold.

"And brutal as it is, unjust as our people may be at

times, hasty and cruel, I feel they are creatures of light and joy compared with those whom we awakened in that deep chamber."

"Yes," said Arbold. Nothing more. In the time he had been possessed by the lyre he had understood many things, only wisps of which remained with him now. Nevertheless, he was overcome by a deep feeling of depression and dread—not for himself, but for the world he had left.

After a time, he stood and gave his hand to Enid. She looked back at the weapon that lay in the grass. Then she shrugged and followed him down the pebble path, around the little lake into which a fanciful fountain tinkled, and out the open gate into the street beyond.

Arbold stopped short on the stone-paved path. The way into which they had emerged was bathed in the full glare of noon sun, which stressed the tawny skins and golden eyes of the people who walked there. Enid caught his hand, and he gave hers a squeeze before freeing his own to hang carelessly beside the worn blade at his side.

Three young men were approaching them. They were strung out into a line, talking intently and making gestures with their square hands. One of them glanced at Arbold as they neared him. He stopped short, catching one of the other two by the elbow. Then all three bent amazed and questioning eyes upon the two who stood by the gate into the garden.

"You're not a Hasyih," said the first, quietly, and it was no question but a statement. Then his eyes fell upon the lyre as Arbold shifted it in his grip.

"The Key!" he breathed. "Come, if you will, with us," he said to Arbold, and though it was courteously spoken, the soldier knew that it was more command than request.

He shrugged, turned to Enid, who smiled faintly and said, "We are fortunate to have found guides."

They went, then, quietly and quickly, through a city unlike any that either of them knew. Yet it was not totally unfamiliar, for though it was built of pale stone, it was formed into gentle curves and smooth arcs and flows much like those about the tower they had left.

Arbold moved through the serenely busy streets, yet his mind was worrying at memories of tawny-skinned people frozen for eons in the deeps of the tower. There was no doubt. These were of the same blood. Even the city was akin. And the eyes in the cold tubes had been evil.

VI

A tower rose before them. As they moved nearer down the curve of the way, its twin bulked behind it. Their pale shapes were crowned with scarlet roofs that burned in the sunlight.

Even as they neared the low stair that led to the doorway of the first, there came a disturbance within. And as Arbold stood in the portal, lyre clutched awkwardly to his chest, a fleet figure swirled toward him down the hallway, calling backward to an invisible presence still upon the stairs behind.

"You felt the return of the Key, true. But I, dear

Neryi, felt something infinitely better. Dead though he may be, the spirit of my friend is near. Hurry!" So saying, she turned toward the bright doorway, her emerald skirts billowing about her light feet in a sea of motion.

When the light touched that dearly familiar face, Arbold felt his heart lurch against the tightly held lyre. He set the thing gently against the wall and held out his shaking hand. "Child?" he said, so softly that she was not sure she heard.

Then those green eyes were squinted against the light, the strong and slender hands were gripping his shoulders, turning him so that the scarred and puckered face was brightly illuminated. He closed his single eye and felt unbidden tears trickling down the side of his nose. Then his arms were about her, and she was crooning to him as though he were now her child.

Finally Enid laid her hand upon his shoulder and brought him back to himself. Holding the girl away, he looked her up and down.

"This is my young scamp," he said to Enid. "Make a nice curtsy to Enid, who is a lady of much courage and wit," he said to Yinri, who obeyed immediately, much to the disturbance of her attendants, who were now crowding into the hall.

And then Neryi was with them, at last, and Yinri caught his arm and led him to Arbold. "This, my husband, is the only father I have had since I was tiny," she said. "Dear Arbold, this is Neryi, who is my lord and friend. And my name, that was lost long ago, is Yinri."

Neryi smiled, his golden eyes absorbing the two strangers in his hall, his inner hearing humming with things unsaid.

With a gesture, he thanked and dismissed the three guides. With another, he set servants to scurrying to make up rooms for the newcomers. With a third, he swept his wife, Arbold and Enid with him into the small chamber where Yinri and the Children of the Asyi had rested, so many months ago.

"Now," he said, when all were seated and provided with refreshments, "we can unravel this strange skein. Firstly, friend Arbold, how came you by the lyre?"

So Arbold told his tale, simply and clearly, and all the while his shrewd eye was examining this stranger who was, suddenly and without warning, wedded to his child. When he told of finding the lyre in the willow, Yinri leaned forward, eyes wide. And when he described the city of the tower, with its powered lighting and moving rooms, Neryi frowned, his lips set. And when Arbold told of those who waited, frozen, in those depths, he sighed so deeply that it was almost a groan.

Enid set her goblet on the table before her. "I have been thinking and worrying, all the while, about a thing that frightens me. It seems that my man and I, unwittingly, started the things in the tower to working again. By this, did we bring those in the deep chamber back into life? They strike terror to my spirit, for they breathe of evil. We loosed danger into the world when we took refuge in that tower, didn't we?"

Neryi reached across the table and touched her hand.

"Feel no guilt, Lady. Though you may have set it into working a little earlier than intended, the power that operates the tower never dies away entirely. When my folk, and those *are* of my folk, evil as they were and will be again, go into their long sleep, they set automatic safeguards to bring them forth again within a given span of time. If they set the time for so great a span, then it is certain that they worked havoc in your world before your remote ancestors were born. And if they are, indeed, awake now, they will work more.

"They were our kin, long ago. They sought after powers that they were unfit to hold, and they courted potencies that befoul any who use them. For this reason they were banished from our world. We thought them dead, for our fathers tried to stop every doorway leading from the Heart of the Worlds into yours, which is the only one of all the impinging dimensions holding a world supporting life. Evidently there was a door that was not found or stopped, and Koyil and his crew went through to devastate an innocent place.

"This explains the foreboding that I and my kindred have felt since Yinri woke us from our long sleep. When Koyil wins free from the little death, he will be, after all these millennia, still set upon revenge against us. He was one who did not forgive and would not forget. He will come against Hasyih, soon or late, and if you had not come through the door that the lyre made for you, we would be unwarned of our danger.

"We cannot know when or how that danger will

come, but now, at least, we know from what quarter to expect it. As well . . ." and Neryi's golden eyes were somber ". . . as the forms it may take. My people have not always been wise. They have made weapons too dreadful for use, but Koyil, I do not doubt, will use them."

Arbold sank back in his chair. "I am glad that our coming has helped you," he said, "but I still wonder to find my child a queen."

"It seems, Arbold, that the child you loved and saved is the offspring of one of those whom Koyil took into Ranyi. Only that can explain her. She is the Queen of Hasyih, with all the wisdom and power and inherited memory that such an one must have. We wrought well here, but if those who wake in that ruin survive their awakening, and if Oramphis is able to find and to aid them, then our work has not yet begun."

Yinri was frowning, only half listening. When he paused, she asked, "How is it that I have been here for almost a year, yet Arbold was but a few days' journey behind me? He accounted for only a night and part of a day in the city. Another day upon the river. Let us say that he was about a week or a bit more in getting here. Where did the time *between* go?"

Neryi laughed. "Search your memory, my love. Surely among the things that the other Yinri has stored in your mind is the fact that time *here* and time *there* are different. Not always holding the same difference, mind you, but never moving along a concurrent track.

Which means that if fortune and the gods smile upon us, we will have opportunity to deal with those who walk a world they have no right to own."

Arbold had been listening, frowning with concentration. "Who, then *is* this Oramphis? You talk as if he were in this place, yet we saw him—or one like him —in the tower. A thin, white-faced fellow with black eyes. He was leading those folks from the forest, urging them on as if he held some power that they feared and trusted."

"He was here," said Yinri. "He crawled away . . . but you have not heard my own tale. It was thus . . ." and she proceeded to tell him the story of her journey that led her into Hasyih. She touched but lightly upon the goings from place to place, but she slowed to give great detail of her finding of the lyre and what came after.

"The same willow!" exclaimed Arbold. "The one that leaned like an arch over the path and out over the water? In the little clearing with the flat stone?"

She nodded, and her tale continued. So when she came to the place at which Oramphis had crawled away into the crowd, Arbold was nodding.

"Had had the run of the place, all the secrets in the temple. He likely had doorways located in many places, so that when it looked best to run, he could go where none would think to follow. And that door may have led him into the very wood about the tower. Think what those in the forest would have thought to have a man come tumbling out of nothingness at their feet . . . he could have persuaded them that fire was ice."

Enid spoke now. "They would have thought, with some reason, that he would be able to overcome the fire-blades that Urthant and I used against them. And he could hardly have known what the tower-city held within its walls.

"Which causes me to wonder . . . one of those weapons lies, even now, in the small garden in which we landed. It is dangerous. Someone should bring it here. I had an aversion toward touching the thing again."

Neryi gave a slight start, then sent one of his Silliyi running to retrieve the thing from the garden. "Touch it lightly, Oyi!" he called after him. "Only upon the smooth tube, not on any account on its stock."

"So you know of the weapon that breathes fire?" said Enid. "I had wondered if such still existed, even in memory, in this peaceful place."

"Peace is not a permanent ornament of any place," answered Neryi. "The Queen and I have spent many busy months in returning Hasyih to something like its ideal state. But there were weapons before, there are now, and sadly will always be. We allow no armaments more deadly than bow and blade and spear, but within this Temple there are vaults sealed with strange locks and binding oaths. There, other things live in well-deserved darkness. My kin, who are the Children of the Asyi, are entrusted with their secrets. Only we, and the Queen, of course, have entry there.

"You see, there are Guardians . . ." and his voice trailed off.

Now Oyi returned, carrying the unfamiliar weapon with caution bordering on terror. He laid it upon the low table at Neryi's elbow and saluted, his boyish face flushed with his haste.

"Thank you, Oyi," said Yinri, smiling, making his face turn a deeper shade. "You may go." As his footsteps clicked away down the hall, she turned a wicked glance toward her husband, and Neryi sighed with patently assumed irritation.

"This child of yours has the entire group of Silliyi madly in love with her," he growled to Arbold. "They fall over their feet; they forget their orders. All she has to do is smile or speak kindly to one, and he grows red enough to set aloft on the signal peak. Yet I find that Hasyih is the richer for her presence."

He leaned forward and took up the weapon, holding it lightly by a metallic band halfway down its stock. "This is the safe zone for this particular weapon," he said to Enid. "I don't know how well you learned to use them or how much you worked to learn their operation, but each one, at some point upon its hand grip, has a plate or a band of this gray metal. It is well to know, for carrying one about in an active state is a perilous thing."

"We learned that much, at least," she said. "We went among the racks, finding those that would work for each of us and committing their appearances and positions to memory. It was well we did, for the first time the forest people came, pretending friendship, we were given little time to comprehend their true mission and arm ourselves. Had we not known exactly what to do, we would have died, Urthant then and I a bit later. Yet I have never felt comfortable at the touch of the things, and I have never learned to live with its effect upon flesh."

"It is an ill thing," whispered Yinri, and for a moment her eyes were old and full of pain. "My ancestors played with dire toys in the youth of the world, and these are of that kind. There was a strain of bitter cruelty in my folk, and those whom you found frozen are their near kindred.

"After a time—a very long time in men's terms—the vitality left the line of the kings, and they died away. Yet there in the world from which we both came, the seed still persisted. Some one of those exiles forsook his or her kind to mingle with the native people. And so I was born, to stand in the keep yard and be saved by Arbold. To find the lyre and to return to Hasyih at the precise time when Oramphis was busy reviving the old evils, whose histories were stored within the temple.

"Oramphis taught the short-lived folk that the gods were myths told by ignorant primitives. He tried to erase the knowledge of their works in Hasyih. Yet they are working, even now, to form their patterns and to shape their wills upon this, which is the Heart of the Worlds, and the world that flows outward from Hasyih as petals grow from the center of a blossom."

She blinked, then shook her head, as Neryi watched with his quizzical expression. "That other Queen speaks through my lips now and again," she explained to Arbold and Enid. "It is a strange sensation to remember things you never experienced, to see things you never saw."

"And now it is time for our guests to rest," said her husband.

Arbold nodded, and Enid looked about at the others, slowly and consideringly, before she said, "We, too, have been placed in the spot where we are needed. I take it that we will join our minds and our hands together, seeking to solve this strange dilemma?"

"We will be happy to have your help," said Neryi, rising. "But you must rest well, or you will find yourselves unfit for the work in hand. And Yinri must rest, also, for in some months we will have a child—another green-eyed witchling, I hope. It rests ill within me that we must cope with such problems at a time when all should be peaceful for her."

"Well, the gods must have meant it to happen," said Yinri mischievously, "though you and I had something to do with it, I will admit. And we *knew*, Neryi, that it was for more than the simple ordering of this little land that I was sent into Hasyih and you and your kin were waked from your long sleep. I have been wondering and worrying all this time, longing to find out what the large task might be. Now that I know, I can go about my work with an untroubled mind."

"Women are like that," said Enid, chuckling at the strange look upon Neryi's face. "Things that you expect to frighten them they notice little if at all. Things that you hide from them are the very things they will be happier for knowing. But you can never know in advance. My poor Urthant gave up, at last, and treated me as if I were another male. It works better in that manner."

Arbold reached for the lyre, which he had set beside him upon a stool. As his fingers touched it, it glimmered strongly, gave a quivering note as if of farewell, and vanished.

"Ah," said Yinri. "So it did before, when it went from me to you. Into whose hand is it now delivered? I wonder . . . I wonder . . ."

But there could be no answer.

The Rune
of Enigmas

I

THE LYRE glimmered, green as willow leaves in the dark corridor. Around the curve of the hallway, a dim sparkle of light still quivered, but that little light did not dull the green glory of the thing that waited, hanging in the air from some support not tangible in this world.

The slap of sandals fumbled toward the spot where it waited, and the form of Oramphis, still clad in grimy white, moved into view. A tiny swarm of notes still bobbed about his head, but they were dying away, one by one, as he came. He held no torch. Those who had followed him evidently still slept, for none came with him.

The lyre pulsed with joyous green, hanging there at just above head-height. Then the man's black eyes caught that emerald glint, and he stopped. Several deep breaths he drew and expelled, trying to bring himself into focus again. But when he looked, the lyre still hung within his reach.

Unbelievingly, Oramphis reached upward. The lyre dropped smoothly into his hands, as if it had been waiting only for that. Trembling with fatigue, eagerness, uncertainty, he touched the strings, and a strident ripple of music followed his fingers.

Immediately, the corridor was bathed in white light from panels that curved away down the center of its ceiling. The throbbing that had vibrated the tower grew deeper, stronger. There was a whisper of sound just around the bend, and Oramphis slip-slapped toward it, the lyre gripped tightly to his thin chest.

A small, dimly lit room opened into the corridor. It emitted a light hum that seemed to compel the wizard toward it. The lyre hummed in a similar key, warningly, but the man ignored it and entered the place. At once, the door whished shut, and the floor fell away beneath his feet. He fell to his knees in the center of the room and bowed his head over the lyre. Sweat dripped from his lank black hair and crept down his scrawny neck.

The downward journey was not very long. The motion stopped; the door opened again. The man rose unsteadily and stepped into the blackness beyond. With terrified awe, he looked about for a way of escape. Running his free hand over the surfaces beside the room, he touched a plate beside the door. Light bloomed coldly in a straight-walled place. Such light as he had never seen, even in Hasyih.

Wide doors stood closed before him, and Oramphis went toward them, pulled in some inexplicable way by the strange throbbing of the building about him. He was stiff with fear, and his soul writhed within him, yet a compulsion beyond breaking gripped him. Something urged his hand to release its grip upon the lyre, but the fingers seemed carved of stone about its frame, as he approached the doorway.

One narrow door opened inward. Without any action on his part, light came again into being, and he

stood in a great square chamber. Across it was another
door, and to it he went, stiffly as a puppet.

It was not locked. He opened it with a push. Terrible
blue light sprang into being in the room beyond, and
he could see immediately the tall tubes, the tawny figures
within them . . . the waiting, watching eyes that shone
triumphantly golden in that frozen light.

He cried out, and the lyre struggled in his grip, as if
to break the spell upon him. But the emphatic throbbing
of power rose through him, and his right hand rose to a
bank of colored buttons on a panel beside the door. It ran
across the thing, touching intricate sequences. A galaxy
of colored lights sprang into being on a glassy plate
above the panel, their hues and patterns shifting as his
fingers moved. The light in the place changed, losing its
blue tint, warming toward rose. The wisping mists of
cold that scarved the tubes grew more dense, more active, until the whole room was clammy with their
breath.

Now Oramphis stood motionless, the lyre clasped to
his chest as if for protection. With growing terror, he
watched the subtle changes in the forms within the
tubes. Strong red light had filled the containers, and
warmth was interrupting the eons-old chill of the air in
the chamber, making the mistiness of the air even
thicker. The very stone of the tower seemed to throb
with effort.

The forms in the tubes were now almost hidden in
the curdled air, but the frightened necromancer could

still see their outlines. Those were now definitely moving: a shoulder shifted here; a head tilted there. The golden eyes were invisible, but he felt them staring toward him, even through the fog. When the mists began to thin, Oramphis crouched beside the door, with his face on his knees.

The lyre dug into his chest, but he paid no heed. It hummed faintly, but its vibration was lost, now, in the clamor of the power machines below the tower. Yet even above the uproar, the man heard the first of the tubes open, its sibilant *shish!* cutting through all. He shuddered and dug his face against his thigh bones.

He felt, rather than heard, the being from the tube come to his side. He understood, without hearing a word or any inward thought, that all the will beside him required him to rise to his feet. His clammy hand slipped from the lyre, and it slid downward to lean against the wall. He rose unsteadily and nerved himself to look, at last, into those fearsome eyes.

II

Koyil stood, once again, within the Cold Chamber. The stiffness of unknown centuries hindered the movements of his bones and muscles, but the ferocious will that had taken Hasyih to the edge of destruction, that had moved his followers with him through a totally unsuspected interdimensional doorway held him straight and arrogant as always.

He frowned at the grubby figure beside the door. It was none of his own kind, sallow and dark-haired as it was. One of the native-grown stock, most surely. Yet not a primitive. There was a glint of understanding behind the terror in those black eyes that told the Hasyisi much. He fumbled in his still-benumbed memory for the tongue that these cattle had spoken in the days before dire necessity had sent him to the little death.

But the other forestalled him. Its terror was subsiding, and it had the temerity to look him in the eyes and to say, "I speak the tongue of Hasyih quite well. I was High Priest there for several years."

Koyil did not reel with shock. He had never done so, and even this astonishing statement caused not so much as the twitch of an eyebrow. Unlikely as it seemed, on the surface, the fact remained that pure and idiomatic Hasyisi was coming from its lips.

"I will accept that, for now," he said, his voice rumbling unfamiliarly in his breast. "Now you must assist my people to awaken. Mine is the only tube that opens of itself. Had I died in the little death, it was my will that all of mine must follow me. Now I am needful of slow and deliberate movement to wake my nerves to full capacity. You will be—convenient—for my purposes. Go!"

Oramphis, would-be Lord over Hasyih, Messiah of the wild woodfolk, moved hastily to obey. Not in the most dreadful nightmare of his life had he envisioned such an intolerable situation as the one that now engulfed him. Yet he knew that any hesitation, any fumbling on his part, would likely cause his immediate destruction. There was about the tawny-gold man who stood flexing his arms and legs, arching his back, an aura that promised much, and all of it dire.

He tugged at the lever that sealed the second tube. It was stubborn with long disuse, but he moved it at last. The tube *shished* open, and a tall, slender woman stepped leisurely out of it. Her golden eyes were mocking and contemptuous as she regarded his form, his face, then dismissed both from her attention and turned to approach Koyil.

One after another, he freed the people from their long captivity. Ten men, there were, and eleven women, and all moved at once to join their leader. When they stood together, crowding the end of the room, stretching, flexing, moving in effortless unison, Oramphis looked upon them with renewed terror. These were no sort that he had ever seen or known.

In all his time in Hasyih, the Children of the Asyi had never waked from their own long sleep. They would have given him some yardstick by which to gauge these who were their age-old kindred. But he had regarded them as myths. Even when they stood on the tower beside that absurd child, he had thought them no more nor less than those whom they called the short-lived ones. Now he was faced with twenty-two enigmas, and his corrupt soul shuddered sourly within him.

The room had now become almost overly warm. The naked golden bodies glistened with sweat, and a strange, bittersweet pungency touched the air. Oramphis felt wetness trickling down his own back, beneath his robe. His knees were trembling, too, but when Koyil gestured peremptorily, he scuttered toward him.

"In the outer chamber there are chests. In a red one, you will find clothing for us. Bring it!" he told the terrified man, and Oramphis hurried to obey.

When all were robed, the women in emerald, the men in scarlet, Koyil surveyed them with satisfaction. From a wall cupboard that had seemed to be only a part of the plain wall, he took out ivory wands with smooth, carved patterns on their handles and tips that flickered with blue fire when they were held. Each of the Hasyisi received one and tucked it away beneath the robes, which were fitted with loops of gold thread for the purpose.

"Go and prepare food!" he commanded Oramphis.

"I beg your forgiveness," cringed the wizard, "but I am a stranger here. I do not know where there is food, nor where there is fire on which to prepare it. I was led here against my will, in spite of the lyre, and I am not certain that I can even find my way back to the world above."

"Lyre?" boomed Koyil. "What lyre?"

His eyes were scanning all about the room, coming back to the thin man's figure, examining it, then moving on. Oramphis, having retrieved the thing upon leaving the room of the tubes, now held it hanging from his left hand. Koyil's eyes crossed the space where it hung without a trace of reaction.

Oramphis, for the first time, felt a stirring of hope.

The lyre, though it had proven to be his enemy in the beginning, might now be his friend. If the Hasyisi could not see it, did not know that it existed, then he had a weapon left. If only he could find the way to use it.

But now Koyil was losing his patience. "We will go together. You will be shown your duties. Do them well." There was no provision made, Oramphis noted, for his doing them ill. As he knew himself to be inept at any work done with the hands, he shuddered faintly. He could call the ravening powers from their dens of wickedness and harness them . . . somewhat . . . to his will. He could direct and misdirect men in many activities. Cookery, however, was a thing done by invisible minions in unseen regions. He knew only the outward appearance and the flavors of its results.

Koyil ignored the moving room that still waited, humming faintly, in the corridor. Instead, he led the group, followed by the reluctant Oramphis, to a ramp that slanted steeply upward.

"Our bodies are stiff and unwieldy. We will climb, giving our muscles the work that they need," he said, and not one of them objected or questioned.

Though the downward journey had seemed short in that little chamber, the way upward seemed endless. Time after time, the ramp turned upon itself and began another upward tilt, leaving behind layer after layer of closed doors and dark corridors. Oramphis slapped along in his worn sandals, his calf muscles cramping and his back weary past belief. He had never valued physical strength for himself, and he found time to regret his long years of sitting in record rooms and bending over study tables.

They reached their destination at last, though he would have passed it without recognition. The band of light that the lyre had activated had died away after he left the way. Koyil renewed it with a sweep of his hand against the wall plate, and the light came again just as one of those whom Oramphis had led against Arbold and Enid staggered groggily into view.

Koyil looked at Oramphis. Oramphis said, weakly, "I brought him from the forest out there . . . with others. We were hungry, and those who lived here would not give us food."

Koyil's thick red-gold brows assumed a skeptical twist. However, he said only, "We do not need him now," and aimed the wand at the startled man's head.

He went down without a sound, and Oramphis had no notion whether he were asleep or dead. The little cone of light still danced at the wand's tip, however, and he said nothing, made no sign, just went where that wicked finger pointed and opened the door into the chamber where Enid had done her cookery.

III

Koyil stepped once again into the laboratory and looked about him. It was evident at once that it had recently been tenanted. It was equally evident that it had been used for homely tasks, not for its real purposes. He sighed with relief. There had been the tiniest wisp of uneasiness as he wondered if some of those who were

his kin and his enemies might have traced him to this
world.

Without his giving any direction, his people went at
once to work. They searched out the visible cabinets,
finding none of the stored goods left except those in containers that were obviously defective. Then they activated mechanisms and hidden cabinets opened. In them
were white canisters and dark bags that proved to hold
fruits and vegetables preserved in their own juices, as
well as dried meats and herbs. But the dried stuffs puffed
into dust when they were removed from their bags, and
by that the Hasyisi knew that their little death had been
long, indeed.

Still, there was more than enough for their small
number. With disgust, Koyil discovered that the man
who had freed them knew nothing about being a servitor. He was clumsy with his hands and his motions. It
was necessary to tell him how to open the canister, to
show him where utensils were kept. At last, Koyil lost
patience.

"If you cannot be of use to us, then you must cease
to exist. I will not be troubled by your presence," he
boomed.

This time Oramphis stood his ground. "You have
forgotten something," the dark man said. "I have stood
in Hasyih within the past month. I know what is happening there, at this moment—at least, I can make some
very accurate surmises. I know that you are of their
blood, and I suspect that you came here in much the
same way that I returned to this world, by way of the

hidden doorways. I would say that you have been here, locked away from the happenings of your native place, for centuries . . . perhaps more.

"I know that a woman has come—a child, really—and all say that she is the Queen Who Is to Come. I know that the Children of the Asyi woke at the time of her coming. Since I was engaged in . . . practices . . . that they disapproved, I left soon after their arrival in the city. Still, I know many who are yet there who are my sworn allies and students. I am a key, Great One, to Hasyih as it now exists."

When he fell silent, Koyil looked closely at him. Those black eyes held the arrogance that the old dark wisdom carried with it, it was true. The hands and the body were most certainly not those of one who was of any physical use in the world. Koyil made one of his swift and effortless decisions.

"We will read him," he said, and two of his associates caught the man by his skinny arms and bore him smoothly to a tall white slab that stood in one corner of the chamber. They touched a button, and the slab slid aside to reveal a man-shaped indentation, into which they pressed the resisting Oramphis. Clamps slipped from the sides and held him tightly in their chilly embrace.

Teeth chattering, Oramphis managed to cry, "Had I but one of my pupils to stand beside me, I would call out the old powers and shrivel you where you stand. I have manipulated the dark forces!"

Koyil grinned. "So have I," he remarked carelessly.

"But I had intelligence enough to recognize that they were too dangerous and erratic for any man's purposes. I gathered together those of like minds, and we built things of glass and metal and artificially-formed substances that would work our will without thought or protest. We can curl a city into blackened ash within ten heartbeats. We have done it, here on this world where we stand. We can cause any building to erupt from the inside, flinging contents and tenants outward with the force of its explosion. We have no need of your demons!"

He gestured, then, and a cone of hot orange light shot down to bathe both man and mechanism in its rays. The slab slid back into place, covering the place where Oramphis stood, but now it was transparent, in some eery manner. Through it the man's shape was a shadow. Even the blood that moved through his veins showed as minuscule pulsing filaments. The activities of his brain were clear, also, and upon a plate above his head the electrical impulses that it emitted were inscribed.

One of the tall women depressed a key, and another hum began to lend its harmony to that of the other mechanisms. After a short time a ribbon of some thin substance began to creep outward from a slot beside the key that she had touched. She gathered it as it came, coiling it neatly. When there were several yards of it in her hands, she tore off the strip and took the coil to Koyil, who began at the end and examined it closely.

Before the strip had ceased to move through the slot, Koyil had read all that he had in his hand. He only glanced at the rest of it, a hint of his sharklike grin showing at the corner of his wide mouth.

When Oramphis had been removed from the machine, Koyil sat upon a stool and looked at his thin and wavering form. "So now I know you, Oramphis of Elthinas. I know why you were forced to find the resonances that would admit you to the safety of Hasyih. I know why you searched the records so carefully in the archives of the Temple, pinpointing the outlet *here* of every door *there*. You cannot afford the luxury of going, ever again, to Elthinas. You are convinced that the very mountains would topple upon you, the lakes rise up to drown you . . . and it well may be that they would. I would not gainsay it.

"I know what you did, what you caused to be done, in Hasyih. Even though I was cast out, my kindred hoping that I would die with my followers in the southern forest, I can find it in my heart to resent your . . . practices. You followed in my steps, true, but you did not understand my motives. I wanted power, and when I found that the black evils held no secure basis of it I abandoned them. Only a few of the short-lived ones were sacrificed to my purposes.

"You were possessed by the sheer love of that dark filth. How many of the lesser Hasyisi did you sacrifice to your lust?" The quiet tone in which he had begun to speak gave way, at the end, to booming anger, and Koyil sat for a moment, regaining his composure.

Oramphis, for once, said nothing. His pale face was now deathlike, and he swayed as he stood. The lyre,

which he had let fall from his hand before being shut
into the mechanism, he had regained by pretending to
fall to his knees when the slab was removed and the
clamps loosed. But now it seemed a hope so slender as to
be almost invisible. The power that Koyil and his folk
wielded made the tiny abilities he had wrested from the
Dark at the cost of so much pain (to others) seem like
the game of a child. Bitter envy wrestled with sick
despair in the devious runnels of his mind.

Most abhorrent of all the unpalatable facts he now
mulled over was the certainty that the lyre had not
been sent to him for his own purposes. Those Who Pattern the Worlds, jibe at them as he had done, had sent
their own instrument into his hands for their own in-
scrutable reasons. Evil though he was, Oramphis was
not in any manner stupid. He knew himself to be situated so that he must play the game of the gods to save
his life. The thought filled him with a wrath that almost
blotted out his terror.

This moment, he felt in his bones, was the hinge of
his fate. In the next few heartbeats Koyil would conquer
his anger and find uses for his captive—or he would not.
Oramphis clenched his teeth together to quiet their clat-
tering and stood as still as he could manage.

Those golden eyes were glittering, deep-buried
under red-gold and bristling brows. The other Hasyisi
were silent, seeming hardly to breathe.

Then Koyil spun the stool about so abruptly that
Oramphis jumped inside his skin.

"Confine him. He may be useful to us if we find

that we must approach those within Hasyih. The state of this world is unknown to us, now. At least we will know the conditions of that one."

Clutching the curve of the lyre with desperate fingertips, Oramphis followed the tawny and scarlet-clad figure that beckoned to him. At the moment his most urgent concern was to conceal the fact that he held something that none of the Hasyisi could see. He went into the small chamber they indicated with something like relief, even when he heard the door sigh shut behind him with grim finality.

He sank upon the metallic chair beside the sleeping couch and tucked the lyre into the curve of his shoulder. With his right hand, he touched the first string, delicately as he was able. The string glimmered mockingly as it vibrated to his touch—soundlessly. No whisper of music did it emit.

The man slumped. Wearily he set aside the instrument. Then he rose and touched the plate as he had seen the Hasyisi do to produce light. The bright illumination died, and he fell onto the couch with his last strength. But even in the darkness the shape of the lyre shone green and silver, and he heard the mockery of its voice in the dark turmoil of his dreams.

IV

The Hasyisi needed no sleep. As did their distant kin, the Children of the Asyi, they slept for millennia and waked for centuries more, if that were called for. Now they worked almost frantically in the laboratory, testing

concealed switches, checking intricate systems for de
terioration, activating perceptors all over the abandoned
city.

They were accustomed to waking and finding
change. Still, Hasyih was a stable place, almost the only
one in an unstable universe. Such change as had come
upon this other world in the time of their little death was
not within their experience. The city that had stood
upon the riverbank amid grassy meadows was now sur
rounded by a forest that almost rivaled the southern
forest in their own world in its forbidding air of age. The
city itself had crumbled and worn away in many spots,
walls falling to ruin, roofs sinking beneath the weight of
the years.

Even the stone with which they had caused the way
to be paved was runneled, as much with the rains of age
as with the footsteps of men. They stood before their
vision plates and scanned the city, street by street,
though some of the perceptors were evidently broken
in the falling of the buildings that held them. Nothing
living broke the pale sameness, except for scrawny blos
soms that had found footholds in cracks and crevices.
They stood in a dead city, surrounded by wilderness.

After a long time, during which they examined every
part of the city that was still observed by their devices,
Koyil stood and said, "We shall see if the remote percep
tors are still operable. There is nothing here worth our
attention."

Before they could move to do his bidding, there was
a faint babble of sound from the corridor without. Shout

dimmed by the thickness of the wall, thumps and sharp blows against the stone drew the Hasyisi to the doorway. Koyil took his wand from its loop; then he moved to the door, and it swished aside.

Those who had followed Oramphis milled in the pitchy hallway. For them there had been no silver-noted lyre, no journey in a humming chamber. They had waked to total darkness, confused and lost. No leader had answered their cries, and there was none among them capable of conquering his own fears enough to pull the group together. Their wild eyes, glistening and beastlike, turned toward the lighted doorway.

Something between a wail and a growl rose from their rank, and the Hasyisi looked upon them with contempt. Koyil swept his wand upward, and the cold flame licked wickedly from its tip. As he moved it from side to side, however, that flame became a wide beam of blue light. Before it, the men fell once again into unnatural sleep.

When all were quiet, the Hasyisi walked among them, counting and evaluating them as a careful farmer does the beasts in his herds. There were a dozen of them, thin and worn-looking men for the most part. Two were women, however, gaunt and somehow tragic figures with scars to match any of those on the men. All were clad in hit-or-miss collections of ill-fitting garments made of rough-spun stuff or animal skins. They were, quite plainly, living in the forest on a level little, if any, above that of their fellow tenants, the beasts.

Koyil regarded them with distaste.

"If those who survived our . . . error . . . have come to this, they are hardly worth our time," he said, turning one of the women over with a toe. She was thin and shapeless as a plank, her hands brown claws at the end of arms that were all skin and corded muscle.

"Repulsive as a she-wolf," he muttered disdainfully. "Drag these into one of the storage rooms." And the wordless and obedient Hasyisi obliged him immediately.

Alone in the laboratory, Koyil busied himself with the hidden circuitry that controlled the remote perceptors. He had little hope that many—if any—would still be operable, but he felt that venturing out into a world populated with feral beasts such as those in the storage room might be unwise. The Hasyisi, after all, were limited in number.

A range of colored lights snapped on upon the panel before him. He began testing switches, depressing them according to their colors. Switch down, light blinks; switch up, light steady. One after another passed the test, until the entire panel was lit to his satisfaction.

Now the other Hasyisi filed silently into the room; their figures in the scarlet and emerald robes moved as precisely and elegantly as if they were engaged in some quiet dance. Seeing the panel glowing, they went wordlessly to their own posts, unforgotten in the long span of sleep, and activated their own switches and screens. The room filled with multi-hued glimmers and glows, as the systems were tried and found operable.

"We will try for the small installation that . . . stands . . . to westward, beyond the river," said Koyil.

Hands moved, coordinating circuitry and power. A large screen flashed into life above Koyil's head, spanning most of the end wall, though its existence was not observable until it was activated. It glowed a steady bluish-silver, and a subliminal hum radiated from it.

Koyil adjusted the controls under his square hands. No ripple of life, no blur of shadow moved on the bright surface. Added power affected it not at all. The screen pulsed with life, but that remote perceptor was dead.

The Hasyisi moved his hands again, and the screen winked out.

"We caused that complex to destroy itself, if my memory serves me," the tallest of the women said. She spoke confidently, but her eyes were fixed upon Koyil, and her knuckles were white in her lap.

Koyil grunted. His own memory, thus jogged, served up the same fact, augmented by the recollection that he had caused this to be done as a lesson to those of his companions who had escaped his domination. They had set up strongholds of their own, and he had had no intention of allowing any rival power to contest his own will upon this convenient world to which he had fled.

"We will try our hidden armory to the north," he said shortly.

Again hands moved, lights winked and steadied, the screen glimmered. The hum rose . . . and bands of shadow rippled across the panel.

"Something is there!" exclaimed Koyil, and his fingers danced across the array of buttons and switches.

The shadows formed and flowed, then steadied. The

Hasyisi gazed at the picture upon their wall, eyes gleaming strangely in the reflected light.

The perceptor was angled oddly, showing the corner of a square-walled court. The pale material from which the place had been molded was crumbled, in spots, to rubble, and in the gaps thus provided grew rampant weeds, bushes, and even small trees. The wall into which the perceptor had been set had evidently shifted with the loss of its abutting supports.

"Shift to the one within the shielded chamber," commanded Koyil, fingering his buttons.

"Will there be light there?" asked the tall woman, who, being his consort, was the only one of the other Hasyisi who dared to question his decisions.

"The wall will be down," he said. And it was. The inner perceptor was placed as it had been, but the wall it faced was tumbled inward, and the rubble that had been flung into the shelter of the chamber had been marked by flame.

Within the range of their vision was most of that wall, together with the depth of the chamber between. The floor was littered with rubbish. Among the stony debris, the creeping tendrils of vine, and the collections of windblown leaves were shapes that made the Hasyisi catch their breaths and clench their fists against their thighs.

"Could they—oh, Lord Koyil, could those weapons still be used?" asked Inyit, who had been his lieutenant in the old days.

"They were made to outlast men and kingdoms," the

Hasyisi answered dourly. "A few centuries . . . or even millennia . . . of weather and vermin cannot quench their fires. They pose no threat to us, foolish man. The creatures who spawn on this world have not the wit to recognize them as weapons, else they would be elsewhere. If no weapon were to be seen there, then, indeed, we might have cause to fear."

"But who, then, cracked that shielded keep?" asked Aniyi, his consort. "If the primitives had no knowledge of its contents, why should they waste their lives against its fierce walls? And if they did not . . . then who?"

The question winged silently about the room. There was but one answer.

"We did not succeed in—eliminating—those who broke faith with us," Koyil said, his voice heavy and gruff. "Some survive yet, it may be, out there in that inhospitable world. Or their children's get. It is unlikely that they could have found a way to enter the little death, surrounded as they would have been by ignorant natives. Without such a period of resting, they could not have survived many centuries. The question that must now be asked is this: Did they teach their young the secrets of the Hasyisi? Did those children breach the armory and remove from it enough of the *other* weapons to make themselves secure?"

To that there was no answer.

V

Oramphis woke, slept again, and woke again before anyone thought to bring him food and water. Isolation, along with the fear of starvation, worked to shake the arrogance of the Elthinan. Those whom he had freed were potent beyond any living beings he had ever known. That total confidence of unlimited power cowed him as he had never thought to be cowed. Before it, his own pretensions and machinations seemed the games of a puling infant.

So it was a different Oramphis who greeted Inyit, who came bringing food and drink. This Oramphis was afraid, and fear multiplied his slyness and filled him with discretion.

"We cannot trouble with you each day," Inyit told him. "This will have to suffice until we think of you again. I counsel moderation." And with that encouraging advice, he was gone and the door hissed shut.

The Elthinan clenched his jaw until his teeth hurt. His hands, however, held the bowl and jug carefully, bore them to the table and set them down. Dried fruits, strange-flavored and -textured bread that had all the satisfaction to the tongue of a puffball, meat that seemed mummified. But edible. That, with water, must be his ration for days, perhaps. He looked about his prison and gave thanks that, at least, he had light. Such a captivity, in darkness, might well drive any man beyond the edge of sanity.

So he endured. The lyre gave him no help. He could not even while away his long hours with strumming, for its strings only shone with silver laughter, never emitting a sound. The events of his life were not such as make good company in solitude. Recounting them could give no comfort at all, yet he found himself reliving old angers and lusts. His time in Hasyih was, in a way, less terror-filled and more terrible than any other part of his strange life.

He mused, there in that old tower, upon that other tower, the temple, where he had found stores of history, of theory, of arts both graphic and arcane. The story of Hasyih had known dark chapters, he found, and those who had written them had recorded their deeds, their methods, and even their thoughts upon the matters.

But the power! He had had the vision to perceive, as those foolish Asyi had not, the infinite array of potencies thus revealed. Dangerous, indeed, was the seeking; but the reward was well worth any risk. He had chosen his acolytes and the Silliyi of the Temple with extreme care, that no word of his endeavors might be breathed to the more traditional of the Hasyisi. Most of all, he had guarded against revealing his works to Yinom, knowing that the king was no fool and no villain.

It had been his good fortune that Hasyih was no cradle-safe spot, stable though it had been at the heart of the chaos of worlds. Men—and women—moved about the land, attending to trade, to agriculture, to herds and to the mines in the mountains. The dangers of the southern forest were not unique. Each portion of Hasyih had its own perils, and many who went forth did not return.

It had been a mere matter of choosing which of the outgoing citizens to waylay on his journey. The forces that fueled the dark power fed on life . . . and on fear. A strong miner delighted them, or a fierce shepherdess.

They lasted long, and the fear of the strong seemed to be more nourishing than the puny terrors of those already afraid. So he had picked and chosen, feeding into the black vortex that grew in the temple the strongest and best of the wayfarers of Hasyih.

Long before the return of the Queen, there had been an unrest in the city. He had known it, and his henchmen had sniffed about for its sources. But the Hasyisi were not primitives. They, short-lived or no, were the heirs of millennia of culture, tradition, and intelligent direction. When evil entered the city, they sensed it, below the realm of consciousness. As the force in the temple had grown more focused and eager, the folk of the city had grown wary.

At the last, he had grown afraid of that force, even he, whose work that darkness was. A moil of terrible power had surged within the well of the temple, sucking warmth and strength from all who came near. The Silliyi had feared it, though he had warped their minds and their wills to hold them to their task. His acolytes, weaker folk than the warriors, had died, one by one, leached to bone and nerve by that hungry force.

And still he had walked about the city, with high and low giving him civil greeting. None had suspected that the malaise that gripped Hasyih was his doing. He had attended upon the King, from time to time, being treated as one who deserved deference. It had fattened his self-esteem . . . and it had overblown his confidence.

Knowing the ways of priesthoods in Elthinas, as well

as other places within his own dimension, he had assumed that the entire mythos concerning the Children of the Asyi was typical priestly misdirection. As for those six who purportedly slept until need awoke them—even the young of his own world would have been skeptical. He had discarded all the rules and the prophecies, assuming them to be as false as those he taught in their places.

Now in the confines of his small room, he admitted to himself that he had been in error. By bounding that other world within the familiar perimeters of his own, he had forfeited the game in Hasyih. The actual appearance of the Children of the Asyi, together with that strange waif who evidently *was*, incredibly, the Queen Who Was to Come, had flung him from his normal state of balance.

So when he had been brought to his knees by the King, when even the cloaking favor of Syim was no longer of any use, he had crawled away, as ordered, escaping the dreadful eyes of those who had stood upon the tower top. Yet he had not gone alone. Syim, knowing that the Children of the Asyi had long suspected his character and motives, had broken from his guards. Both had reached the concealment of one of the many gardens of the city.

With the instinct that causes a wild beast to bury part of its kill for the future, Oramphis had sent Syim into a state of trance, from which he could be waked, even after weeks or months, to a condition much resembling his normal one. Scuttering through the streets as if he were a rodent, using every concealment and secret way that he had learned in his years there, he had spirited Syim into the very lowest cellar of the temple and had there hidden him away. So long as that weak and wicked man lay sleeping in Hasyih, Oramphis felt, he had still a weapon there, however unlikely.

His own escape through the doorway that he had chosen long before was a simple matter. But he had come back into his own moonless world filled with bitterness and wrath. His rejection by his own people in Elthinas had rankled less. That had been well-deserved—the penalty for losing the perilous gamble that he had made there, with the priesthood of the entire land the prize for winning it.

It was another matter entirely to be cast out by those whom he had reckoned to be fools, easily misled down fatal pathways. Sitting in the inhuman light of his prison, Oramphis mulled sourly over his miscalculations in Hasyih. Had he only known that the unlikely tales in those jewel-records were true! Had he only realized that in Hasyih it never occurred to any in a post of power to falsify the chronicles of their country! If he had only sought out the Children of the Asyi, wherever their sleeping places might have been, and slain them as they dreamed! Without their aid and counsel, the Queen would have been vulnerable. Even with the lyre . . .

And his eyes slid again to that strange instrument. It leaned against the wall beside the table, its strings winking wickedly in the cold light. Compelled against his willing, he reached for it, and it settled into his arm comfortably. His right hand touched the strings; and for the first time since he had freed the Hasyisi, the thing spoke its bright notes.

They swarmed upward from his plucking fingers, shining motes of light more vital and even less human than the light that filled the chamber. In swift and disciplined ranks, they flew outward, caromed from the walls and the ceiling, and bounced back to settle about Oramphis in a disciplined vortex of energy.

His hand moved on the strings, though his frightened will sought to still its motion. More notes and more joined the throng that now swirled so closely about him that he felt stifled. His heart thumped painfully, and his face grew hot. The hand strummed on, and even the left one would not release its grip upon the frame of the lyre.

He stared downward at the greenly glowing shape. Two runes now were incised into its greenbone frame. The key-rune at the top had been joined by a sword-rune. Though Oramphis had seen it only briefly and at a distance before it came into his own possession, he felt dimly that there was a difference in it. But the runes gleamed enigmatically, and the would-be wizard played on, possessed by the power of the thing.

Now he fell into a dreamlike state. Fear left him. He no longer fought his steadily moving hand. The notes vibrated about him, holding his fogging eyes, and their resonances permeated his mind and his body. The overriding arrogance and ambition that had borne him through his life were soothed into slumber, and his naked spirit was left to steep in the essence of power that was the music of the lyre.

VI

The Hasyisi had not been idle in the weeks of their newly awakened life. Those wild creatures who had followed Oramphis into the tower had been set, by twos, into the mechanism that had "read" Oramphis. Only the first two had been scanned for their knowledge and experience. Inyit, given the task, had reported that though their potential for intelligence was not low, their rough and disrupted lives had channeled their minds into the most rudimentary levels. Simple survival was their experience and their purpose.

Therefore, they and their companions had been "written" instead of read. The commands of Koyil had been imprinted on their consciousness by the machine. Then they had been released into the forest, free to follow their own ways until an inaudible signal from the tower might recall them to the service of their new masters.

While that was being done, Aniyi and Koyil busied themselves with testing out, slowly and carefully, every remote scanning device within the tower. Those in the laboratory were but a few of the mechanisms that had been set to observe the world for the Hasyisi. Even upon the other continent that the planet held, they had set their spying perceptors, though the inhabitants of that land were the gentlest of forest folk, without, they assumed, the skills to work metal and minerals into weapons.

High in the tower, in a chamber that occupied the whole of its tapering top, had been placed an entire complex of panels and perceptors. From that nerve-center, Koyil had been able, at a touch, to look with his own eyes upon any spot on Ranyi that he had judged sufficiently interesting or dangerous to receive his spies. Now he tried, often in vain, to reactivate the system.

Many of the perceptors showed them familiar places that were overrun with unfamiliar folk and totally alien styles of living. Indris, the nearest of the smaller strongholds, now held no being who remotely resembled those of their kindred who had built it. Gardens grew lushly where the training fields had lain in grassy-neat precision. Families dwelled in the cavernlike structures meant to house the power systems that had evidently never been installed there. Laundry flew its multicolored flags from the walls and the low towers.

Aniyi, knowing Koyil for many lives of common men, held her tongue, making no comment or suggestion as to causes. The veins on the man's forehead were growing distended. His eyes had sunk deep beneath his red-gold brows.

As one after another of the holds came under their view, Koyil grew more dour, and the air about him seemed charged with wrath. Every place that they or their rebellious kin had built was tenanted now by those who had been the simplest of peasants when last they had looked upon them. And they were prospering among the ruins the Hasyisi had left; their activities were intelligent and well-directed. Even the marks of war that lay about many of the holds only showed that those whom the Hasyisi had scorned as cattle had now developed into full-fledged men, with all their follies. Those pitiful few who lurked in the forests about the tower were evidently outcasts and misfits, unrepresentative of the state of their fellows.

Koyil ground his teeth together. "It was no plan of ours to bring them to this condition. They were biddable beasts . . . and so they should have remained. The forces we unleashed upon those of ours who defied us should have driven these vermin deeper into beasthood. How could this have happened?"

Emboldened by the question, though she knew it to be purely rhetorical, Aniyi ventured an answer. "The forces we unleashed, Koyil, Lord, were ones with strong and immediate as well as subtle and far-reaching facets. We can see plainly that many generations of their kind have lived and died since we went into the little death. The breath of the power that we loosed may well have worked upon their lines of heredity, forcing them, untimely, into their own future. I think that we have none to blame but ourselves for this unlooked-for progress."

She saw his face darken with anger, but she had said what was in her mind, and she now closed her mouth and smiled secretly as she bent over her instruments. Not for nothing had she spent a thousand waking years in his company.

"We must break them back into the dust," he said harshly, switching to another scanner. "Even if we must rebuild those dreadful weapons we used before." He saw neither the council room of the hold he sought nor the humming blank that denoted an inactive perceptor. The panel before him darkened almost to black, and upon it sparked forth myriad points of silver light that moved in intricate patterns, which changed from formation to formation, disciplined and precise; below, in his prison chamber. Oramphis touched the lyre.

Koyil's eyes narrowed, and he tapped the buttons before him, seeking to clear the panel, to eradicate those unlooked-for motes of interference. They persisted, untroubled by his machinations. With logical progression, they circled, opened into blossomlike concentrics, flowing into helices, independent pools, ellipses. There was more than beauty in their motions. There was meaning that spoke to some unverbal sense within both of the Hasyisi.

Their eyes were fixed upon the panel. No act of will could wrench them away, as both Koyil and Aniyi found upon trying. Those delicate ranks marched and countermarched, ebbed and flowed, engraving silver lines upon something inside each of them that seemed a blank placque, ready for etching.

They sat, enspelled, for an uncounted time, unaware. The day dwindled, and the moonless night made no distraction. Others of their folk came, at times, and called softly at the door, but so fearful were they of Koyil's wrath that none dared to open it and to look

within. So they remained through the night, and when
morning peered through the eastern window, the pane
glimmered its last, and the moving silver motes winked
away.

Aniyi moved, stretching her back and arms. Something felt strange to her, though she could not have said
what it was. Beside her, Koyil sighed heavily and rubbed
his strained eyes.

"No response?" he grated, surprised at the rough-
ness in his throat and the unused-feeling in his voice.

"I must have slept for a time," she answered. "Yet
I think that we found nothing. Let us stop and go to
nourish ourselves. I am more weary than I should be, so
soon after the little death."

He grunted and rose, but his eyes turned to the pane
again, and there was a spark of unease, a hint of con-
jecture in them. Then he shrugged and turned to the
door.

"Strange," he said. "I am fit to drop with weariness.
Are the years at last beginning to take their toll?"

As they moved through the doorway, the room behind them darkened, and on the now-invisible panel a
mocking handful of silver points dipped and spun.

VII

When every perceptor had been tested, every dis-
cernible part of this world examined as well as it might
be, Koyil was less than happy. Fewer than half of their
remote implacements were in order. Yet the holds that
were under their surveillance were tenanted, if at all

inhabitable, with swarms of sleek and busy folk. The smaller continent, where the Hasyisi had made their strongholds, was burgeoning with new people who were making new directions for their lives.

The great sprawling continent that was the sole other land mass on Ranyi still hid in unbroken woodlands. The few installations there were in most part workable, and they showed the same shy beings who had always lived there. No untoward industry thrived there, no expanded fields and improved strains of livestock. No looms powered by the wind or the flowing of streams. No light, distantly akin to their own cold illumination, powered by the muscles of sturdy peasants on treadmills.

For the Hasyisi the thought that others might reinvent their own techniques for power and fabrication was one that rankled. In all their long lives, none excepting only they and their immediate ancestors had molded metal and glass and fiber to create the things they willed to exist.

The notion that these primitives of Ranyi had managed, in a few short millennia, to arrive at the principles that underlay most of their own techniques was one that both angered and frightened the Hasyisi. Only one thought possessed them all: If they were again to dominate this world, it must be returned to its former state. The folk must be made again into frightened and biddable cattle.

"Each hold contains the seed of its own destruction," mused Koyil, holding a metallic map over a frame, below which the cold light beamed. The incised markings were cast into bright focus, as he traced the positions of the places that he must destroy. "They are all within range of the great weapon, and it can cause them to erupt into force and flame, if we so will it."

Aniyi murmured, "Yet it seems a pity . . ." before being caught up in the tempest of her spouse's wrath.

"Pity! Pity is the maundering of the fools who now hold Hasyih. Pity is for the weak and impotent. We, who are the highest achievement of the Asyi, the only wielders of true power in the history of Hasyih, are not formed for pity. These vermin are a danger to us and to our purposes. They must be cast down from this inappropriate pinnacle to which they have stumbled by chance. To serve our purposes they *cannot* hold themselves to be true men."

She bit her lip and stared down at the map, but her heart, so long asleep, seemed to have wakened to more than ordinary sensitivity. She knew, deeply and without doubt, that the course Koyil proposed was wrong . . . wrong and, quite possibly, perilous to his own kind. But she said nothing. From long experience, she knew that Koyil could not accommodate the thoughts of anyone but himself.

"We shall demolish their holds now," he said, more to himself than to her. "Then, if they still prove intractable, we will loose the poisoned breath. Better no slaves than recalcitrant ones. At the least that will leave us a secure base from which to retake the overlordship of Hasyih."

Aniyi looked up. He looked, as always, at no one,

gazing toward invisible goals that only he could envision. The set hardness of his golden eyes, the rocklike tilt of his square chin told her that this was another of his iron-bound determinations, and she moved quietly from the chamber, while he was caught up in his bloody dream.

Though she had followed him for untold centuries, never hesitating nor doubting in her wordless obedience, some strange content of the air of Ranyi, some element in its soil seemed to foment rebellion in her. She wondered if Inyit or any of their other companions felt such stirrings. She regarded herself with both wonder at her daring and loathing for her former submissiveness.

Yet, with all her determination to thwart Koyil, she had no inkling of the course to follow. Any of the others might well turn on her with anger and contempt if she questioned Koyil's authority. Within herself, she had few abilities that did not require linkage with Koyil for their usefulness.

There was only one living being still within the tower who might be an ally. Oramphis, she judged, would have no cause to love Koyil . . . or her, of course. Still, if she approached him properly, it was just possible that she might enlist his aid, whatever that would be worth, in saving this planet from destruction and the foulest and most suffocating of deaths. Whatever quarrel Oramphis had had with his native land, he surely must have some regard for the planet that had brought forth and nourished his life. Or so she hoped.

Now she rejoiced that Koyil's Hasyisi had spurned

the old abilities. Had they retained one fragment of the mind-contact known to the Children of the Asyi, she would have been lost. Her treachery would have broadcast itself to everyone in the tower. As it was, Koyil's unshakable faith in material things worked as her ally.

The corridor was empty. Those that wrapped the tower above at every level would also be empty. Koyil had ordered all except his consort to put their equipment in perfect order, preliminary to beginning the destruction of the holds of Ranyi. If only he did not take undue notice of her absence, she would have a time sufficient to sound out their prisoner.

At his door, she flashed the tip of her wand in a coded pattern, thus unlocking the door-opening mechanism. Then she set the wand's beam at its narrowest focus and played it in a circle on the face of the door, just above her own eye-level. As it moved, the stuff of the door grew pale and quivered into transparency. Through a small and temporary window, she looked into the chamber.

Oramphis sat on the couch, still and straight, as though he were waiting. His face held no expression, his hands lay quietly in his lap, his feet were set squarely on the floor at right angles to his calves. He gave the impression, had she known enough of the ways of men and of the gods to read it, of an instrument waiting for use. She could not see the lyre that lay at his side, though she felt a queer certainty that something ailed the light as it struck the fabric that covered the couch.

Satisfied that he was neither disturbed nor dangerous, she opened the door and stepped into the chamber, her wand at the ready in case of some untoward reaction from the man.

He turned his head and looked at her. In the cold light, she saw his eyes, and their expression troubled her, though she could not have said why. After looking at her for a heartbeat or two, the Elthinan rose, straight up from those planted feet. His hand clasped the lyre, though she saw only that he held it awkwardly.

With almost a creaking of hinges, his jaw moved, and his voice, long unused, said, "What would you have me do?"

Aniyi blinked. Nothing in her experience of dealing with ordinary, mortal folk had prepared her for such a reception. How did he know that she wanted him to do anything? For the first time in her over-long life, the woman considered the possibility that her kind was not the all-knowing and omnipotent race that it had considered itself to be. Something else, she felt in her innermost being, had already tampered with this prisoner, who had been kept so closely and so alone.

She shuddered involuntarily, and the man's cold, glazed eyes noted it, dismissed it. Conquering her unease, she said, "Oramphis, you have little to lose. Koyil is preparing to destroy first the holds that still exist on Ranyi, then all the life that remains outside this tower. Though I have followed where he led, always, as have Inyit and the others, now I feel compelled to set myself in his path, to stop him or to be trodden under. I have no idea what aid you might offer me . . . or even if you care enough for those of your native world to try to save them.

"Still, lacking any other ally, I have come to you for help. Will you give it to me?" She waited calmly, her golden face paled to cream, for his answer.

"I am here for that purpose," he said, and those black eyes that had been wont to dart suspiciously around and about all his surroundings were now steady. His awkwardly thin form was held straight, poised firmly on his feet, sustained by some preternatural balance that made it seem almost that he might draw up his feet and still stand securely.

"What . . . "Aniyi whispered, backing toward the door.

"Who, not what," answered Oramphis. "And that, too, will be answered. Go back to your place. I have been told what is being done. Leave me free to move through this tower, and what I can do will be done."

VIII

The tower thrummed with power. The harnessed sun-fires that lived deep beneath it had been connected to every generating device the place afforded. The Hasyisi stood in the high chamber, each before a screenlike panel, each controlling ranks of buttons and levers. They felt the fabric of their clothing crawl on their backs, the hair try to stand erect upon their heads. Even to them, the sensations were unfamiliar and eery, for never before had the full capacity of the tower been utilized, even when Koyil had ordered the first destruction of the holds of Ranyi.

Aniyi, despairing, stood at her post beside Koyil. If Oramphis proved to be useless, as she feared might well be true, her only recourse would be to encode her own controls so as to divert their energies into a counterflow. Even one twenty-second of the power that now flooded the tower should be enough to remove it from the face of Ranyi in a fairly spectacular manner. But she shivered internally at the thought. She loved life as only a near-immortal can do, having much more to lose in death than ordinary folk. Still, she held herself ready, and she gave no sign of her distress to alert Koyil to caution.

Every perceptor was locked onto one of the surviving holds. Busy figures moved in the squares, streets and courts that they revealed. Geese picked and gabbled along the gutters, pigeons swooped across the roofs, dogs and cats and chirrikas went smugly about their business, dodging boots and slippers and barrows and cartwheels.

On Aniyi's panel, a curving court was centered by a wide fountain in which three women battled their laundry against the white stone of the curb. Aniyi could almost hear their babble of talk, as their busy hands scrubbed and batted and wrung the soapy garments. Inside her head, she could see the next few moments . . . the implosion of the central tower, whose top rose just above the wall to her left, the ferocious winds that would sweep the walls inward, carrying with them the women, the wash, to be dashed to bloody smears against the rubble. Something hot rose in her throat, and for the first time in her life she felt the sensations that would accompany the deaths of those wholesome and hardworking dames.

"Activate your preliminary systems," boomed Koyil's voice.

About her, Aniyi felt the activity of her peers. Her own hands moved, but her systems were placed into a holding mode, ready to be thrown into counter-action when it seemed necessary.

For the first time in centuries of waking life, she spoke, internally, to the gods. "Send help, You Who Pattern the Worlds. You must exist, for without you all is darkness and destruction. Give Oramphis wisdom and power. Give me the courage to work my own death, if it be necessary. Help me to save those short-lived, unsuspecting folk from the doom that Koyil intends."

Now the Hasyisi were setting their systems into the first phase, and the hum of their individual machines was lost in the terrible roar of power that Koyil was forcing from the central systems below the tower. The floor, stone though it was, trembled beneath their feet. The walls of the chamber vibrated so deeply that Aniyi felt they grew transparent at times, giving her a glimpse of the corridor, the farther wall, and the noontime sky beyond all.

Behind her, as she sat at the very end of the arc of Hasyisi, the door of the chamber whispered open. She did not hear it, but she felt the stir of air and turned her head cautiously. Then her golden eyes widened.

Oramphis stood in the doorway. He held the lyre

. . . and now it glowed green as summer willow, silver as truth, and she could see it as it lay against his shoulder. In point of fact, his thin, erect form seemed dwarfed by the instrument.

"Now!" boomed Koyil, his voice rising triumphantly above the roar of power.

At the same moment, Oramphis touched the lyre, running his fingers down a complex pattern of notes.

The panels, which had held the horizontal patterns of preliminary mode, flared sun-bright; then they all shattered with the sound of stone crushed beneath iron. Koyil whipped about, his golden eyes seeking for the cause of his frustration.

What he saw stopped the violent words in his throat. Aniyi, wife for ten thousand years, stood beside the scruffy Elthinan, her face vivid with triumph. That absurd primitive dominated the room as if he, not Koyil, were the master of the dominant race in all the wheel of worlds that invisibly surrounded Hasyih.

And in his skinny hands was the lyre. That last and almost forgotten instrument of power had been, in part, Koyil's own. He had lent his hands and his mind to the working of the Queen in her quest for its components. He had, himself, used its potencies in many ways. He had forgotten it—or had it forgotten him?—when he first deliberately rejected the teaching of the gods. The lyre, key and weapon and ultimate enigma, was within his own innermost stronghold, its green fires pulsing to match the increasingly desperate throbbing of the power systems.

Silver notes filled the room like a swarm of bees, and where they moved the mechanisms died. When the last had been eliminated, the two men stood within arm's length staring with desperate attention, each at his enemy.

"I have denied the gods!" cried Koyil. "I have decreed that only I may hold power!"

"I hold the lyre," answered Oramphis, with total calm. His quiet voice pierced the clamor of the laboring generators without effort.

"I have claimed this world for my own. I will subdue it and turn my mind to Hasyih! No native of Ranyi can frustrate my will."

"This world is called by those who belong in it—Ranuit. Remember that!" snapped Oramphis. "Also, take thought of this:

"Your will to destroy those who live here is now frustrated beyond the possibility of alteration. You cannot destroy them, for the lyre has destroyed your instruments. You may do as you are able with Hasyih, but this world you will not shatter again.

"You may, if you will, die here and now. Your power mechanisms have been forced beyond their limitations and have run wild in the roots of this tower. No act of yours can stay them from removing this city, this tower, these Hasyisi from Ranuit.

"There is only one alternative. You will swear the only Oath that your kind keeps that you will leave those of this place to their own devices—body, mind, and spirit. You will not enslave them; you will not seek to do them harm in any manner; you will set no devices to shatter their planet. You will not interfere with their business, their contrivances, or their ways. If you do this, the lyre will channel away this mad river of power into another place, where it will harm none.

"The choice is yours, and you must make it now. Your long lives, Hasyisi, will end within a few seconds, if that is your decision."

In his dirty white, Oramphis glowed with power borrowed from the lyre, as he stood before the Hasyisi. And they, staring at this ragtag nothing that had set their earth-shattering works awry, thought frantically.

But Aniyi was the only one of them upon whom the air of Ranuit had worked its miracle of freedom. The rest were unwilling to die for any reason . . . except for Koyil. His unobstructed will being his reason for existence, he was quite content to die with his illusion of omnipotence. Yet twenty pairs of golden eyes were now turned upon him. Twenty wills, not by one and one the equal of his own, but all together quite sufficient, compelled him to bow his leonine head in a grudging nod.

"I take Oath, by the Fathers of the Asyi, by the Long Waters of the north, the Strange Forest of the south, the gates into otherwhere, that I, Koyil, with my folk, will abide by the words spoken by Oramphis and will in no way compel or influence the folk of Ranyi—Ranuit. In return for all our lives." So he spoke, and as he ended the throb of laboring mechanisms eased, the prickle of force against the nerves grew less. One by one the generating-engines below were disconnected from the source of their power, and that power itself was damped to its normal levels.

"A sun will burn infinitesimally brighter for a day," said the voice of Oramphis, idly. "So much for your terrible powers."

Now the lyre grew brighter, yet. Oramphis shifted his grip as though it were also growing hot to the touch. His whole form began to flicker with green tongues like flame; it grew misty, as the Hasyisi watched.

Aniyi, seeing no hope for herself in the eyes of Koyil, reached out her hand and took the man's sleeve. She, too, began to ripple with green light.

They stood together, Oramphis, ex-priest, defiler of the Temple, slayer of many, tool of the gods, and Aniyi, Child of the Asyi, consort of Koyil, unquestioning instrument and mutinous wife. The glow became too bright for eyes to bear, yet Koyil seemed unable to look away.

In a shimmer of green-gold and white, the two quivered madly, the basic motes of their beings vibrating to powers unnamable. The lyre moved, of its own, from Oramphis's grasp and hung in the air above them, its steady light illuminating the true nature of that below it.

There was one note, deep and bell-like. The two winked out as though they had never been, gone to a refuge only Those Who Pattern the Worlds could know.

The lyre hung above Koyil as if it were staring at him. Another note, high and bright, thrummed from it, and far below them Chirri, the little beast lost and left behind by Arbold, found his own door and entered it joyfully, leaving behind a long span of loneliness and hunger and darkness in that vile tower, to enter a forest world where he might be safe and happy.

There was one note more, and with its going the lyre itself was gone. The chamber was dead about the spot where it had hung. No sound came from panel or button or lever. Only the normal indefinable hum that was the life of the tower moved in all the place.

Yet there was one source of fury left. Koyil, bereft in one short span of both his inordinate belief in the power of his will and of his wife, burned in the room with force enough to alter the courses of planets.

He said, however, only one thing: "They have left us Hasyih."

And those about him, their brief rebellion done, bowed their heads in assent and murmured, "Truly, they have left us Hasyih."

The Rune
of Answerings

I

THE LYRE sang in the willow. At this point where air and water, sand and stone, reed and tree merged in a focus of natural power, the instrument of the gods replied to the wind in faint hummings and trills. The morning sun slanted beneath the trailing skirts of the willow, lighting the flat rock to amber, gilding the white beach, outlining the minnows that fed lazily at the water's edge. Fat tadpoles waggled vestigial legs among the reeds, wary of the green, glassy water snakes that looped quietly between the tall stems.

The quiet was intense, enhanced rather than shattered by the tiny *lip-laps* of the ripples and the song of the lyre. As the wisp of breeze fingered the harp, wavering shimmers of light appeared and vanished all about the spot, upstream and down, west toward the forest, east across the breadth of the stream.

A twig of the willow bobbed in the wind, touching a string sharply. A shining door appeared between two berry bushes on the inland side of the beach, and out of it walked a tall figure dressed in celestial blue.

He looked about with interest that contained no surprise. Moving forward, he stood beside the flat rock upon which Arbold had sat and gazed with delight at the wavelets of the stream. Then with a sure hand he reached without looking into the willow above his head and lifted down the lyre. Cradling it, he ran supple and knowing fingers over the strings, making them flash brilliantly in the morning light. As if in ecstasy, the instrument responded, sending its bright notes flashing about him.

Playing, he turned in his tracks and walked up the path along which Yinri had skipped to her own errant notes. Ahead, a doorway quivered into being, an arch of vibrant motes dancing just at the stream's edge at a point where it looped sharply. Without hesitation, the blue-clad minstrel approached it and passed through, seeming ready to step forth onto the shining water.

But he walked through it onto deep mold and into darkness that was awhisper with murmurous leaves. The passage through which he had come glowed with green-gold light behind him, lighting the edges of branches and a patch of forest floor. With a final minor note, he erased that corridor between the continents; and with its going the blackness grew complete.

The minstrel did not move nor strike light from the lightglass that hung from a loop of his belt. He sought no shelter, nor did he stretch himself upon the ground to sleep. He simply stood, totally silent, straight and steady as one of the invisible trees that he knew surrounded him, waiting for the dawn that was many hours away. For he stood, as he well knew, upon the other continent of Ranuit.

The night whispered away at last, and the sky, far above thickly leaved branches, turned pale. The beasts that had prowled quietly about the reaches, even about the feet of the newcomer, stole away into their daytime coverts. A bird tried its morning song, high in a tree that was covered with giant scarlet blossoms.

The tall figure lifted eyes as golden as the newly risen sun and looked about him. "It has been long, indeed, since I stood upon the soil of the Forest Continent," he mused, moving his hand so that harp notes accented his words. "I have slept for untold centuries, dreaming worlds and ways and spaces far beyond the limited spans of Ranuit or Hasyih, but none of those were more fair than this place.

"The notes—the notes woke me, as I slept in that strange dimension between worlds. There is a stir in the wind that tells of powers waked to fury and folk moved to action. I have been brought from the sleep of my refuge by Those Who Pattern the Worlds, and they have sent me here."

Now his hand moved fiercely across the glimmer of strings, sending summoning notes dancing away through that great wood. And it became apparent that he had not been talking solely to himself, for swift flashes of coppery skin began to flicker between the boles about him as those who guarded the ways of that subtle continent assessed their visitor.

He crooned wordlessly, now, tickling the lyre to lighthearted melodies, as his inspectors moved almost invisibly through the forest about him, communing with one another and their distant leaders in their wordless fashion. Without concern, seemingly, he waited for their decision, but his hand was never still on the lyre, and its notes went where none recognized them and influenced councils unaware of their presence.

The sun marched up the sky, leaving the tops of the trees and beginning to strike down between their tremendous shafts to spill pools and patches of light upon the deep mold of the forest floor. Into such a patch walked, at last, a small but commanding figure; and when it appeared, the minstrel bent his straight neck and swept his hands wide in a strangely archaic gesture.

She nodded, a slight but civil gesture, and came to stand before him. "You are Guyin," she said, craning her neck to look into his face. "With the incomers you came into this world, full of bitterness and hatred. With them you subdued those who dwell on the far shore and built up cities of unstone and metal. With them you fought, at last, going away from their holds to form your own place with the woman who chose you. This much our sensing has told us, coming through the long time since; all such sensing is preserved in memory, handed down from old to young.

"We have known when you went from this place into that world of sleep that renews your kind. We have known when you returned and found other wives to warm your days. We knew, Guyin, when you died."

"It is true, Mnemora," he said. "Your people's gifts are true and comprehensive. But at the end, it was not death that took me, though I believed it to be so. Those Who Pattern the Worlds took me forth from my burning hold, from the defense of my wife and my child. They thrust me through a door I did not dream existed.

I have lived in dream since that day. Now they have brought me forth again, and it may be that you can tell me a part of their purpose, for your kind is turned to the silent music that runs between worlds."

"Come with me," she said. "We will speak of such things in places unwatched by the eyes of Koyil—if any of those eyes still see."

Startled, he looked down at her, but her face was still and closed. He followed her through the wood, and now he did not play. All about them was birdsong that trilled and fluted and murmured among the trees, seeming to make the blossoms quiver and the leaves to dance with the undisciplined music. As they went, he saw the quiet folk in their green shifts nod to his guide, then to him. They did not follow, but kept their watch.

II

He felt the flow of their thought, webbed through the air like summer gossamers, tickle across his own mind. The eons in which he had denied those archaic talents under the tuition of Koyil seemed, now, to be years and centuries of time lost from the things of importance for his kind. He had always known, in some unsubdued part of himself, that Koyil taught nonsense. Only the presence of Inyis had taken him into that group, and with her appalling death from the sting of an insect, too insignificant to seek out and crush, he had drawn away from them.

He had gone, alone, into the little death; and when he awoke, he had found one of the women of Ranuit to love and to care for. Mnemora had been accurate. For many cycles, he had lived in Ranuit. And he had died there, to be snatched from that narrow way into the very hands of the gods whose work was the patterning of the worlds. That dream-racked span had waked his own intuitions and powers of the mind and spirit. More than that, it had provided him with a body that seemed familiar but was in subtle ways different from that one he had shed when the blade struck home, so long ago. Or was it long? In that non-space that had held him, time did not exist. It might be . . . it might even be that his daughter still lived.

They had moved along tenuous trails through the forest as he mused. Trails so unnoticeable, so natural-seeming that he doubted that he could find his way back again, should the need arise. There were no twisted or diseased trees in that wood: all stood straight and tall and exuded health. All the small beasts that scuttered among the fanlike undergrowth or chattered in the branches above them were lively and bright-eyed, with the smooth fur or the polished scales that bespoke ease of body and spirit.

Now he could see ahead a bright space that seemed clear of the overwhelming vegetation that was the clothing of this continent. A dozen paces brought them to the edge of a small clearing that was laid out as neatly as a game board with squares of cut-stone pools, circles of low dwellings whose thatching was of living vine clad in green-gold leaves and starred with tiny white blooms that filled the air with faint, sweet scent. Geometric patterns of walks connected them in arcs and loops of dark-green mosses, as luxurious to the foot as any man-woven carpet. At intervals the eye sought for relief from the green . . . and found it in artfully natural tumbles of milk-white stone, whose curves and angles satisfied some need for balance deep within the mind.

The minstrel paused, unconscious of his hesitation, to absorb the scene before him. Mnemora smiled a secret smile as she watched his thin face change with the changing patterns of the things upon which his eyes rested. She did not disturb him but stood as quietly as a tree or a shrub, the faint fluttering of her straight robe repeating the motions of the leaves about her.

When Guyin again turned his face to her, it was filled with peace and pleasure.

"I have walked upon this land before," he said, "and another Mnemora spoke with me in friendship. But she did not lead me here. We talked in the deeps of the forest, and she guided me wisely, though I had no claim upon her wisdom or her regard. Her sensings and her words are the reason that my life fell into the lines it took, and I have never regretted seeking her out.

"My kin, there on the broken continent, have never dreamed that this wooded land holds anything worth seeing or knowing. That, if nothing else, proves their fallibility."

"My ancestress left her memories of you, with all else in her mind, to those who came after," said the woman, gesturing toward the path that lay just to their left. As they walked toward one of the flowering houses, she continued, "She thought well of you. Her words were, 'This is an Hasyisi unblinded by folly. Watch him well, and aid him if need be.'"

"She saw more deeply into me than I, at that time, saw into myself," Guyin murmured, his hand touching the lyre strings so softly that only a whisper of sound came forth. "I was blinded—but only for a time. I was foolish, but her advice directed me away from the folly of my peers. So she and the gods who pattern our ways have brought me here to you, at this time, holding their instrument in my hands. And I have no idea what it means. Read for me the state of the worlds, Mnemora. There is need, I think, else I would not have been moved through two strange doorways into your world again."

They now stood before the doorway of the house, and he stooped to follow Mnemora into the chamber beyond. Then he stood again in silent appreciation.

There were few furnishings. A low couch piled with mosses was partially hidden by a curtain of growing vine. A low table was formed of a cross-section of opaline stone, through which a shaft of sun struck down from above, lighting it to splendor. A circular bench of the same substance surrounded it, and the concentric design, the mushroom-shape of the table, the simple curves of the bench supports delighted the eye.

The inner walls glowed with filtered light that twinkled through the thatch, and blossoms were patterned about the walls and the roof, for the covering vine ran in disciplined profusion over all. Nodding toward the bench, the woman drew from a nook in the vine a pitcher of green glass and a covered dish of white stoneware. When this was set upon the table, she sat beside him and smiled.

"There is much need," she said, "for all our thought, all our wisdom, all the power that the gods have placed in their lyre. But first you must break that fast that has lasted for years—few to you, perhaps, but many, nonetheless. And then we will tell you of Ranuit, and of Hasyih, and of the things that we have sensed as they happened there."

Guyin lifted the cup that she had given him, filled it with pale green nectar from the pitcher, and drank with pleasure, tasting the subtle flavors of honey and fruits. Rich, dark bread was beneath the white covering of the bowl, and he bit into it, feeling that he had never before tasted real food.

When he had done, the sun had moved higher in the sky, sending wefts of beam down into the house to light the entire place to beauty. Gazing down into the glowing stone of the tabletop, he said, "There is, I'd warrant, no place quite like this in all the worlds that embrace Hasyih. Yet I find a question: what holds out the rain?"

Mnemora laughed, a rich chuckle that warmed the room. "The vine," she told him, "is adapted to its task, for many generations have seen to its development. When night comes, or when clouds cover the sky, the leaves lie flat, one lapping the edges of the next, making a secure roof. Only when the sun shines warmly do they turn their edges to angle upward, letting in the light and the air. They do not fall, even in the cooler months, but replace themselves so gradually and smoothly that no gap ever appears to let water drip into our sleeping faces."

The grasp of life-forces, the knowledge, and the patient lifetimes of work that he glimpsed through her simple statement left Guyin breathless. He bowed his head for a moment, thinking of Koyil's assessment of the folk of the forest continent. Then he looked up.

"Tell me," he said to the woman. "It is time."

So Mnemora set her elbows on the table, her chin in her hands, and began. "First, you must know that your child lives . . . and now rules in Hasyih," she said to him.

Guyin's jaw dropped. "But only the Queen Who Is to Come can truly rule there," he said.

"You are a Child of the Asyi," said Mnemora. "Your blood carried the heritage truly to your only child. Did you never think it strange that of all your marriages on Ranuit, only the last produced a child? And that that one was left to fend for herself at an age when most are still cosseted in their cradles? Those Who Pattern the Worlds hold stern training for those who are to work their wills. So it was with your daughter, who now is the Yinri who rules in the tower and the temple."

"But how did she find her way into Hasyih? The doors are not open to any but adepts . . ."

"Or to those who hold the Key," finished Mnemora. "And she held the lyre that you now hold. Look upon its frame. You will see runes that were not there when it came from the hands that made it. The Queen whom you served, ages ago, left it plain and unadorned.

"At the top is a key-rune . . . yes, there. Then a weapon-rune. Lastly a rune denoting questions unanswered. It has made three journeys into the worlds, and three sets of hands have used it to further the workings of the gods. When the last space is filled, there at the bottom, I'll warrant that it will hold the rune of questions answered and resolved."

"Then you know what has happened?"

Mnemora nodded. "Thus it was . . ." and she began the tale of Yinri's life after the fall of the hold, her finding of the lyre, and her journey into Hasyih. "There the girl, with those Children of the Asyi who still draw breath there, dislodged foulness from the temple, thereby dislodging its creator, Oramphis. And in that name you will find the key to the return of the lyre into the affairs of mankind. For Oramphis opened a way into Darkness that was, in itself, a trigger that set many things in motion.

"Banished from his refuge in Hasyih, Oramphis returned to this world of his birth, deliberately seeking out a doorway that would set him near the tower where Koyil and his band had set up their holding. He had no knowledge of who and what had formed that city beside the stream, but he had, that one, a feel for things of power.

"And here is a strange bit of this puzzle that we have not yet determined a fit for. Years before, two came there for refuge, fleeing wars in their own places. Enid and Urthant dwelled there, harming none until men came to harm them. Yet we believe that the augmented power that their presence roused in the place began to waken the old Asyi who slept the little death, deep beneath. So it seems to us that, ignorantly, they caused the peril that now threatens Hasyih."

Guyin looked up and shook his head. "No, none can wake us from the little death except our own devices. I cannot know why Koyil set the time for so long, unless his kind had shattered that continent so thoroughly that he was giving it time to heal itself. Yet a limit was set, for who would sentence himself to eternal frozen sleep? It was not coincidence that he began to wake at that time, for to believe that would be to deny the pattering that we can see in all the workings of the worlds. Time came about, and the mechanisms began the slow process of thawing those within the tubes.

"And look you, when those traps opened, there stood Oramphis to puzzle and distract them. There was the lyre, which they could not see, waiting to visit destruction upon them. The most frightening aspect of all is the fact that *only if those within the pattern make the right decisions* will the pattern hold true. Each one of us bears within the ability to shatter the tranquility of universes. So even that necromancer, when faced with the truth of his own soul as sung by the lyre, rose to the level required. Had he been totally unwilling to serve Those Who Patterns the Worlds, he would not have been compelled."

Mnemora's eyes lighted with comprehension. "Indeed! Now it falls into place. We knew that we are not forced to serve, yet we did not apply our own freedom to all. Let us sit, now, and think on what we have learned."

III

Night fell, and the leaves of the roof settled snugly into place. Milk and wine and firm golden fruits were placed on the table before the preoccupied Guyin, but only an apologetic touch upon his shoulder brought him again from his thoughts.

When he looked up, it was into a face unfamiliar to him. A slender boy stood beside him, his coppery skin glowing in the light of a white lamp.

"Mnemora sends her regard. She says that it is time to refresh yourself and to rest. After food, I will light your way to the pools, that you may scrub away your worries in the living water. This couch is yours for as long as you need it, as is this house. And if you need to speak with one of the watchers, or with Mnemora herself, you have only to call, and I will hear." The boy poured a cup of milk and one of wine, broke a fruit and set it on a white-stone plate, where its thick juices began to pool in an amber puddle beneath the halves.

"Thank you," said Guyin, lifting the wine cup and testing the tender vintage. "Your folk have been more than kind to me. Will Mnemora or one of her associates visit me in the morning? There is much to discuss."

"After morningsong I will take you to the house of counsel," the boy answered. "All who are not busied elsewhere will meet together there, and answers will be sought. Though our world is not endangered, Mnemora says, Hasyih is in peril, and Hasyih lies at the heart of the interlocked dimensions. Its troubling, or its destruction, would shatter the laws that bind together that which is. Tomorrow it will be made plain, with the help of Those Who Pattern the Worlds."

So Guyin ate sparingly and set away the food and the soiled cups and plates, then sought his rest. Yet sleep was not a thing he would need for many weeks. He lay in the fragrant darkness, listening to the sounds of beasts and birds that hunted and mated and fought in the black jungle that surrounded the circle of dwellings.

His mind was set in fruitless circles when he tried to think further upon the purpose of his awakening. He felt, dimly yet without any doubt, a sense of doom. All the millennia that he had spent upon the soil of Ranuit had given him a love for the moonless world, but Hasyih was his home. Not until the boy had told him Mnemora's words had he realized how truly it *was* his home. He felt its danger in the centers of his bones.

Koyil, awake and denied his usual excesses with the folk of Ranuit, would have no mercy upon Hasyih. The City, the forest to the south, the pasturelands, the mountains to the north, the farmsteads and townships would mean nothing to his injured pride and his undiminished arrogance. And against that devious, clever and ruthless Hasyisi stood only his kin of the Asyi—and Yinri!

Guyin had avoided thinking of his child, until now. She had been so young, so terribly vulnerable when last he had seen her that the thought of what her life must have been had tormented him. Yet Mnemora had made it plain that Arbold, unlikely as he might have seemed, had been a fit and seemly guardian for the little one until he, too, had been made to appear to die. What strange capacities she had learned, that green-eyed infant, that he would never have dreamed of the need to teach her!

Her mother's face rose into his memory. The polished silk of her midnight hair, the emerald glow of her eyes had been faithfully copied in her daughter. Never again had Guyin looked upon a fair woman with affection after Inyis, but the dark and caring wives he had found among the folk of Ranuit had soothed away the hurt that her death had brought. It seemed strange, indeed, that Laria's counterpart now ruled in Hasyih, the land that had so intrigued the mother who could never even see it.

He sighed and turned his face into the faint fragrance of the moss that formed his pillow. So much that he had accepted without question as unalterable truth was proven to be deepest error. Koyil, indeed, had been a master of folly, but Guyin found that within himself he had always suspected that. The earlier teaching that he had received as one of the Children of the Asyi, however, had never found any questioning in his spirit.

Those Who Pattern the Worlds had found their finest expression in the creation of his kind. So he and all his folk had known to the bottoms of their minds. That unshakable fact had undergirded every act of every one of them, including himself. Now he found that these simple forest people, who lived among uncut forest upon a continent that the Hasyisi had never troubled to name, practiced arts and possessed gifts that equaled or surpassed any that the Hasyisi knew.

Humility sat oddly within him. Its uncomfortable shape prickled at his pride, and he lay in the unrelieved darkness and wrestled within himself. Why, indeed, if the gods could create Hasyih, rising like a little sun among the hidden planets and dimensions that embraced it, could they not make equal sorts of people upon all those worlds? It was a logical question, and he found himself wondering why it had never occurred to any whom he had ever known.

Hasyih was, if truth be known, a wasteful planet. Only within one part of it did purposeful beings pursue their activities. The continent that held the City was for much of its extent barren, sealed away from the fruitful parts of the planet by mountains and a furious ocean. The other two continents were fruitful, in part, with fine forests and lush grasslands, but the Hasyisi had never looked toward them. Their numbers were stable, their needs carefully balanced upon the capacities of their own small place. They had, he saw suddenly, no ambition. Or, perhaps, the sort of ambition that appeared among them was the self-destructive kind that possessed Koyil.

Guyin turned restlessly, his unease of mind communicating itself to his disciplined body. He found, to his astonishment, that he could see, very dimly, several of the white blooms that adorned the wall against which his couch was set. Ranuit had rolled her giant body, and dawn was again touching the sky beyond the doorway.

He rose and straightened the tumbled mosses. Then he looked into the nook from which food and drink had come heretofore, and there he found a white pitcher filled with rosy liquid and two of the covered bowls. He bore them to the table, returned for the dishes and cups that had also found their way there, and saw that those he had soiled the night before had vanished silently while he had lain in his tumult of thought.

The morning was cool, and the pink nectar warmed his throat and tingled down his body. One of the bowls held a warm porridge made of grain, and the other furnished a small melon and an oblong reddish fruit whose freshly broken stem still oozed moisture.

He made an excellent meal; then he called for Aloye, and the youth appeared at the doorway as smoothly as though he had been on the point of entering. Given the abilities of the forest folk, he thought, that might well be true. His intention could have alerted the boy well before he had opened his mouth.

IV

The house of counsel was set at the midpoint of the circular clearing. All the mossy paths wandered outward from the smooth green lawn that surrounded it. And Guyin could see that the entire complex purled gently away from that focus, each dwelling seeming to be a quiet eddy beside the still stream of the pathway. Even the white stone tumbles that accented the foliage and blossoms were arranged with a strange logic in relation to that large round house.

Early though it was, a quiet hum of voices reached his ear as he bent to enter the low doorway. The chamber was filled with green-clad people, their copper skins muted in the dim light beneath the still tightly closed leaves of the roof. With theatrical aptitude, the sun washed over the adjacent treetops just as Guyin entered, and the covering vine responded with magical grace, altering the interior in one long moment from blue dimness to gold-shot green.

Now the faces were all turned toward their guest, and he saw that all had the same large gray eyes that Mnemora had turned upon him. Their hair ranged in hue from flame-red to deepest brown; their expressions varied only in deference to the difference in facial shapes; but their inner selves were blended into one intense aura so concentrated that it enveloped even Guyin's narrower perceptions.

Through the stillness that fell at his entrance came Mnemora's clear and ageless voice. "Well come, Guyin of the Hasyisi. We have joined our minds and our hearts through these dark hours. We have propounded some questions, as you have . . . It shows upon your face; we did not pry into your thoughts," she said gently, as a flush rose under his tawny akin.

"Pardon, Lady," he said. "I have been arrogant and a fool, and the remnants of my folly still cling about me. As well as other things. I must confess to you, before you commit yourselves, that in my long period of unconsciousness I have been stripped of the powers that belong—belonged—to my kind. I can hold the lyre, and it answers to my hand. In that only am I the Guyin who was driven from Hasyih. I have probed deeply within myself, and I find there a place scoured clean of folly, as well as of those things that my folly misused. I will be of little help to you."

Mnemora nodded. "We knew," she said, making a place for him on the mossy floor.

Guyin sat cross-legged, trying to emulate their easy posture. For the first time in his long existence he felt inferior, and he knew, on a deep level, that Mnemora knew that also and was amused.

She began simply. "Will Koyil's followers obey him, even to the destruction of their ancient home?"

Guyin looked at her, surprised. "You believe that they may attack Hasyih?"

"It is in our thought that they may," she answered.

"Then I must say that if there is one who will not follow him, it will surprise me. They have been content to let him govern their consciences for too long to change."

"One alone," murmured Mnemora. "Aniyi, wife to Koyil, has defied his will, saved this world and has gone into otherwhere." Then, as Guyin listened in fascination, she told him the story of Aniyi and Oramphis and the lyre.

He bowed his head. "She was more courageous than I," he whispered. "I knew Koyil to be wrong, yet I followed him because of Inyis, who, in her turn, followed because of Inyit, her brother. We did not allow ourselves to think of the nonsense of his teaching. We were arrogant and all but immortal. We grew careless and will-ful. Each of us lost by it."

He looked about the crowded chamber, the still, bright faces. "Aniyi loved Koyil from the time they were children. She went with him into exile, though it pained her heart. She had been his wife for long and long. I know her reasons, for she was my sister.

"If she turned against his will, it was not for lack of love for him but for horror at something that he in-tended. I begin to understand why I have been sent back into the world of life. Things that were dark are be-coming clear. Tell me what you have thought."

One continuous nod rippled among the heads in the room. Mnemora settled herself comfortably and said, "I am chosen to speak our minds for all on the forest con-tinent.

"Firstly, we ask, with Ranuit foreclosed to him, will Koyil be content to sit in his tower and play with his de-vices? We think not. Do you agree?"

Guyin nodded wordlessly.

"Secondly, will Koyil keep his word to the gods? We have watched him for generations, but we cannot see into his heart. What is your thought?"

"He will abide by his given word," Guyin said, "but it will gall him sorely. His frustration will find a way out, soon or late."

Mnemora bent her head in agreement. "Thirdly, being forbidden Ranuit and its people, having access to no other world peopled by thinking beings, will he not turn his thoughts to Hasyih, that being the root and source of all his fury?"

"He will," said Guyin. "I comprehend now. Having no inner balance upon which to hang wisdom, Koyil is driven by nothing save his arrogant whims. He is not evil, I will maintain. Evil requires a conscious choice of the worse over the better. He cannot make that choice, for his only good is his will, and his only ill is that which frustrates his aims. To my shame I say it: He is as a beast of the forest, without knowledge and without conscience. He will strike out at Hasyih."

There was a murmur through the assembled folk, a sigh more than a comment.

"We have made several premises," said Mnemora. "We believe that Hasyih is the hub and the pivot of an interlocked set of systems, and we fear that any upheaval there will find echoes—perhaps dire ones—in all or most of the others. We suspect that a severe shock there might well find echoes upon Ranuit, physical ones or, perhaps more dangerously, mental and emotional ones."

"Truly, you are among the Wise," said Guyin. "You have read the riddle of Hasyih correctly, though it took my own people many generations to solve. No others of the contiguous worlds contain living beings. There are fourteen interlocking worlds, ranging from barren stone and snow to the lushest of paradises, but only these two, Hasyih and Ranuit, are hosts to animal life.

"We have seen, through the long years of our record-keeping, that when mountains rise in Hasyih, lands shift and oceans spill from their beds on other worlds. So if Koyil strikes hard at my home, your own world is imperiled."

Mnemora bent her head in agreement. "We have given thought to all our alternatives. Failure to act may bring upon our world a cataclysm that might wipe away the long generations of thought and labor that makes the forest continent a place of joy. Yet we also feel for those unsuspecting folk in Hasyih. They have balanced the worlds upon their shoulders, and they have done it well. We would not have them suffer."

The boy, Aloye, spoke from behind her. "We are determined to keep a watch upon Koyil. Those in Hasyih know now that peril will approach them from that direction, for Arbold and Enid have gone through with the warning. They cannot know when it will come, or what method will be used against them. We will be their watchers in Ranuit. We will see, and when the time comes, we will add our peculiar skills to theirs, in order to save both worlds. Does this meet with your approval?"

Guyin looked over the sea of faces. "I am grateful to you," he said.

V

Koyil stood beside the river, his gaze seemingly fixed upon its bright-rippled surface. He was not, however, seeing the water, nor the occasional fish that jumped through its texture after addled insects. For many days he had stalked about the tower, wordless, bemused, frowning. His people had learned to turn and walk away at his approach and never to attempt speech with him. His temper, always uneven, was now explosive.

Nettled at their avoidance, however much he had courted it, he had sought the paved brink of the river by day and the shattered tower room by night. He knew that his thoughts were inchoate as eels in a pond, aimless and unmanageable. No matter how he focused his mind, it slithered unmanageably toward the events of times just past. The bitter fact that he had discounted Oramphis as a peril to his purposes was unavoidable evidence that even Koyil could be in error. And the infinity of possibilities that this suggested was staggering to the mind.

He never moved into the forest that crowded closely to the edge of the stone-paved area. There, he knew, lurked those whom he might not touch, by his own sworn word. Yet those green deeps glowered at him, the glittering river laughed at him, the overarching sky dwarfed him.

Backward and forward he paced, hour by hour, day by day, his heels ringing against the stone with crisp authority. By that one act he held his folk in thrall, still. Had any trace of the inner confusion and turmoil he suffered appeared to them, they would have fled his presence to eke out whatever life they could find among the people of Ranuit. But those arrogant and unwavering footsteps spoke to them in an unworded language, bolstering their faith that was, for the time, without foundation.

Gradually, as day followed day, the inner self of Koyil eased. He regained the power of rational thought, and the first subject upon which he focused it was Oramphis. Alone, the Elthinan could have done nothing . . . at least, nothing truly devastating. Even with the aid of Aniyi he could never have encompassed the destruction of the equipment in the tower. Aniyi's skills were Koyil's own, learned together with him in the training given all their folk. Such sheer power as Oramphis had set in motion was beyond anything known to the Children of the Asyi.

So. There must be, then, Those Who Pattern the Worlds. Not myths formulated by primitives and fostered by the power structure of the Temple. Not vaguely imagined shapes lost in limbo. Actual powers and presences. So he had been taught, surely, but he had thought himself too clever to be caught in traps set for fools. And now he felt himself to be the fool. It was a thing too bitter for imagining.

And Aniyi . . . Could it be that she had drawn apart from his purposes over a long while without his noticing? Truly, a wife who has lived by one's side for millennia is a thing seldom consciously noticed. Trying his memory, he could remember only her look when they had been young. Her mature face would not come clear, only her quiet voice, her infrequent but reasoned points of disagreement. And they had not, after all, been so infrequent. He had thought her rational, but she had been, after all, only a female. Some cyclical insanity had possessed her and turned her aside from his plans.

With that masterly bit of rationalization, he turned his now-clear thought to Hasyih. Now, indeed, he could plot that world's downfall, glorying in the unexpected terror of it.

His head tilted into its old position. His golden eyes glowed with newly kindled fires. With a crash of heels, he strode across the landing and up the ways to the tower and roared into the echoing corridors, "Up from your dallying! There is work to be done!"

One stunned instant of silence followed his words. Then hurrying steps sounded from many directions, and the entry hall filled with his kindred.

"We have waited only for your word," said Inyit, bowing his head.

"You have it," barked Koyil. "Go into the memory crystals and find those dealing with the Banned Weapons. Find also everything dealing with the management of the sun-fires that are our power source.

"We, Hasyisi, are going to recreate those fearful things, mightier than anything we built here before. With them we will burn Hasyih into a cinder, and our vengeance will be complete."

Now there was a longer silence. Those who stood upon Ranuit had come because of their loyalty to this man, but something of each heart clung stubbornly to the Heart of the Worlds, even after so long an absence. For an instant Inyit's eyes rested questioningly upon his master. Then they fell, and he bowed his head again. There was an all but inaudible sigh, and the rest of them followed suit.

VI

The weeks that ensued were frantically busy ones. The knowledge they had pilfered from the storage chambers in the temple, rerecorded in their own crystals and stored in this world against any future need, was painstakingly complete. The Banned Weapons were described therein, down to the last molecule. Their construction, while a thing of great skill and considerable danger, was well within the capabilities of the Hasyisi.

The management of the sun-fires was easy of access, for they had themselves set the forces in motion to power their workings, and those records had been their guides. Still, thousands of years had gone by, and each felt it wise to refresh skills so long unused. Almost without thought, they rebuilt the mechanisms in the tower chamber, for they must be used in delving into the records, as well as in designing their new weaponry.

As if spurred on by his period of inactivity, Koyil was now a whirlwind of energy. In addition to supervising each step of each project, he spent long hours in the tower chamber, plotting his strategy, planning the structures and capacities of his weapons, musing with dreadful gusto upon the last moments of Hasyih. Yet even as he worked he felt at his side an empty space that for years beyond counting had been filled by the presence of Aniyi. Only one spark of warmth had touched his chill selfishness, and its disappearance left an aching gap that no amount of bloody gloating could ease.

Inyit, filling both his own place and Aniyi's, noted his master's strange warmth when they spoke together. From his own loss when his sister Inyis died, he surmised the source of that untoward openness, and he tried to fill the spot at Koyil's side, driving himself to exhaustion in the service of his unnoticing master.

There came a day when the deep reaches of the tower held carefully packaged shapes of metal, spaced widely, one from the other. Shielding swaddled them round, and none entered to inspect them without donning the silver-metal robes that shielded flesh and blood from the terrible breath of those dire weapons. Forgotten telltales in the upper part of the tower sprang into life, tocking away angrily as the concentration of energy mounted, permeating the very stuff of the stone about them.

The Hasyisi, remembering the dangers they had faced in kindling the sun-fires of the tower, were somewhat pale and nervous; but Koyil walked unshielded through the storage rooms, his self-confidence seeming to shed any hazard. The fury of his driving will all but vibrated the air and the walls about him, paling the terrors of the dangerous substances his folk must handle.

When the last weapon was sealed into its canister and bundled in the dull-gray shielding-metal, Inyit and his peers breathed more easily, looking toward a span in which to rest a bit and to gather their wits and their resolution for the great effort that they knew would be forthcoming. While they took their ease, however,

Koyil paced like a tawny automaton, the force of his focused energy nearly too much for his almost-immortal flesh to contain.

With the ending of summer, all was in readiness. The Hasyisi, though most concealed an inner core of sadness, were prepared to destroy the place where their ancestors had first looked upon their universe. Their leader was incandescent with triumphant confidence, and they basked in the strong light of his approbation, thrusting deep into themselves the pain they felt.

Now came a phase of the work that made the breath of sun-fire seem safe by comparison. For the first time in uncountable centuries, they prepared to venture through doorways into Hasyih. In no other manner could they determine where to place their devices, and in no other way could they find the best time to detonate them.

Every door leading from Hasyih into its attendant worlds had long since been discovered and mapped by the Children of the Asyi. A watch was kept upon those that entered from Ranuit into the City, into the lesser cities, and into the villages that lay between them. Only from Ranuit did the people of Hasyih fear danger, and most of those doors were near about the City itself. Only a few, such as that through which Yinri had entered, opened into the wild.

Those were so inaccessible, so difficult of access that Koyil determined to send one of his folk through each of the four that were so situated. Being in places where no people strayed, they were spots into which his Hasyisi might appear without arousing alarm.

So it was that Inyit found himself, had he only known it, standing beneath the very willow in which the lyre had hung. It was late, and the sun was down, only a red glow lighting the sky above the looming hardwoods of the forest. No lyre note might open that way for Inyit—but he had other keys.

He spoke quietly into the deepening dusk, "Ariyin amoyeyi. Ansuyis incalyi eluyir."

He felt the quiver of the air as the door opened up the path ahead, out of his sight among the bushes. Following his instinct, he moved up the dark trail and into the covert through which lay the doorway. In a few moments, he stood on that ledge where Yinri had found herself before him. Now the silver-leaved plant was withered and dry, tanging the chill air with its herbal scent. The forest below was dark-needled, but the last rays of the sun still touched the tips of the tallest of the trees. Here, the day was not so far gone as it had been in Ranuit.

Unlike his predecessor, Inyit knew the southern forest, not well, but enough for survival. No instinctive and other-directed intuitions moved him as they had done Yinri. Only his own purposes sent him downward into the wood.

Among those tremendous trees it was fully dark, and the beasts had roused to grumble and roar and prey upon one another. Yet none of his kind was in peril of creatures that walked in flesh. Another presence haunted the forest in the south, one that none of the Hasyih had ever found definition for. Even Yinri, who was the product of the forest as much as of her own heritage, did not understand what had been done to her in those needled deeps.

So Inyit walked with caution and in darkness, shunning his lightbeam. He wanted no attention from those whom he could neither see nor understand.

VII

It seemed the longest night of his whole existence. Using all of the senses to the fullest, the lack of sight was by no means the disability that it might have been to a lesser being. He bumped his nose against no trees, nor did he fall into fernbeds or deadfall. Still, those same senses told him that he was accompanied, through all that nightmare journey, by those he felt sure would have been invisible also by day.

They frayed at his nerve endings, seeming almost to touch him with intangible filaments. Among the heavy, sweet fall-forest scent there was an alien tang that troubled his nose. His footfalls seemed to whisper overlong before dying away into silence. A bitter taste filled his mouth, unlike any he had ever known. But the stubborn Hasyisi moved to his leader's will, ignoring the presences that teemed in that forest.

He did not tire. Such was the nature of the Children of the Asyi that their long periods of deathlike sleep sufficed as rest, if circumstances denied them other op-

ortunity. In this place, Inyit did not dare to relax mind
r body. Probing forces pried at his mind, even as he
trode through the black deeps, and he locked his
houghts against them. Though he had accepted Koyil's
lecree that the gods were mere figments created by those
vho sought power through the temple, his early teaching
ad been very different. Below the reach of his conscious
vill, there still lurked germs of belief that quickened
ubtly to life, although he did not realize it.

In one night he walked the thickness of the southern
orest, his tough and ancient body, trained through mil-
ennia, bearing him unerringly toward the plain that
tretched away to the City. The rising sun found him at
he fringe of trees that skirted that expanse of grass
vhere Yinri had found Ayilli and his men asleep to the
nusic of the lyre. The silken tent, forgotten, had fallen,
nd the rains and winds of Hasyih had reduced it to a
imp puddle of color.

Inyit paused beside it, wondering at its presence.
Then, dismissing it from his mind, he walked away to a
oll of tumbled grass and lay full-length, drawing the
em of his cloak over his eyes to shut out the sunlight.
He was not terribly weary, but to walk openly across
he open lands was unwise. Not even the simplest shep-
erd could fail to know that he was of the Asyi, and they
lid not move afoot across the lands. Questions would be
sked that could not be answered, should he be seen. So
e lay and willed himself to sleep, as the sun went across
he sky to be swallowed up in a rolling bank of cloud
hat, before evening, covered the sky.

He woke to chill damp as a light mist came down with darkness. Glad of it for its concealment, he wrapped the cloak about him and trudged on. Night fell about him and with it rain came swooping out of the north, the winter wind at its back. He knew that though he had left late autumn in Ranuit he had found winter here, and he marveled again at the incalculable time differential between the two worlds.

He did not slow his pace, however, even as he mused and miles fell away beneath his booted feet, which now sloshed through sodden grasses and softened soil. Still the miles that lay between the forest and the City, which could be passed swiftly ahorse, were long ones to a man's short legs. He felt the dawn, though there was no change in the black sky or the rushing of wind and water. The City, he well knew, was still the better part of a night's march away, so he took thought for shelter and concealment.

It had been long since he walked the ways of his native place. Any cot or sheep shelter that he remembered had long since fallen victim to the gnawing of time. It was impossible to see, even with his other senses, through the wrack that surrounded him. But his folk honored and cherished trees, and a thick belt of them stretched, north to south, between the edges of the grasslands and the farming lands beyond. It would stand even now, he knew, unless fire or storm had destroyed it. So he hurried onward, hoping to come into the shelter of the wood before the coming light betrayed him.

The rain had become visible before he saw before

him a dark bulk that was his goal. Then, among the trees at last, he stopped and drew a long breath. For a moment he was tempted to speak another key and take shelter in whatever world opened to him, stepping back into this after a time. That was not truly feasible, though, for the factor of time lapse differed in all the worlds, and he might return to find that a year had passed . . . or a moment. So he felt among the trees until he found one crooked enough to deflect the downpour, and he settled against its comforting shape to wait out the day.

VIII

Yinri woke quietly but completely. It was dark, still, and the rush of rain sounded even through the thick stone of the walls of her tower home. No sound other than that of the storm moved in the place, but her strange senses told her that something was amiss in the world of Hasyih.

She sat, folding away the downy comfort of her bed-covering, and slipped her feet into the slippers that waited beneath her couch. The winter chill was oppressive within the night-bound tower, but she moved to the deep slit of the window embrasure and stood looking out across the invisible grazing lands. Then she moved about the round chamber that formed the topmost tier of the structure, looking from the window to north, to east, to south.

As a touch against her inner seeing she felt a presence toward the southern forest, the northern mountains. Not the familiar touch of her short-lived folk, nor that of any of the Children of the Asyi, but one oddly kindred, for all of that. Turning, she went to the side of the boat-shaped couch and touched her husband on the shoulder.

He woke totally, for like all his kind he slept only because he might disturb those others who must sleep if he continued his work by day and by night. In one motion he stood beside her, his mind locking easily into hers, sensing her intuition.

"Neryi," she whispered, "it is not one of our own," though she knew that he had grasped that immediately.

"The time is drawing upon us, beloved," he answered. "We had hoped that the peril we all know must come would delay. As all will, who walk in flesh, we had thought to avoid it and to let our successors join the battle. But that is not to be. Those ancient rebels now walk upon our lands, bearing fell purposes in their hearts. Sleep now, for tomorrow we must draw together our kindred and our subjects. War is walking toward us across the pasturelands and the farmlands. We must set our minds, however, reluctantly, to grapple with our coming struggle."

"Yet those who move are only here, surely, to reconnoiter, before the true beginning?" she half asked and half stated, turning from the casement and moving again toward the couch.

"True. Yet, Love, I know Koyil almost as I know my own nearer kindred. Once he finds the things he wishes to know, then he will strike without delay—and without warning. Not for mild faults and small sins is one of the Children of the Asyi exiled from his home.

Koyil is without the communal sensing . . ." Yinri gasped with shock, but he went on . . . "he quenched the gift in his own spirit, deliberately. That was his first and most dire error. He turned from our hard-won knowledge of Those Who Pattern the Worlds, and he took with him those who loved him best. He cut them off from their own people, their own world, and their own better selves. That was his most terrible sin. He dealt unmercifully with our own folk, who are still kin, short-lived though they may be. How do you suppose he has dealt with whatever kind he found upon the world into which he was cast?"

"My world was—troubled. It may be that such was its nature, the nature of its people. But if my father was your kin, as he must have been if I am the descendant of the other Yinri, then must he not have been one of those who followed Koyil into exile? Which means that Ranuit is the world from which our danger will come . . ." Her voice died away as she mused upon the thought. Then she spoke again, with much vigor.

"Neryi, my world ended in horror and bloodshed. Arbold seemed to perish in the same kind of senseless chaos. In every place where I dwelled, there was a tang of strange tension that seemed to come from a place outside its walls. Koyil has contaminated Ranuit. I know it."

They returned to their couch, but sleep was impossible, now. After a time, Yinri spoke into the darkness.

"I know that you are lying quietly, hoping that I will sleep again, but it cannot be. I must rise and go down to the temple, where the records are stored. It may be that some clue of Koyil's purpose could be found there. By dawn, we may have found something to comfort our fearful hearts."

So they rose and moved softly down the chill corridors, the clammy stairways, the dark passage until they found themselves at the door to the chamber of records. Neryi went forward to light the crystal lamp that hung from a wall bracket, and Yinri went at once to the slotted wall and began to run the tips of her fingers along the patterned edges.

First, she relived that painful time of Koyil's discovery and banning. Neryi, familiar with the facts of it, found another crystal and set it into a slot, busying his mind away from the terrible tale that his wife now was learning. When it was done, she rose, pale and thoughtful, to restore the gem to its place.

Between them, the two worked backward along Koyil's earlier life, pursuing every faintest clue to his interests and activities. Before the sun rose behind the obscuring clouds, they had hunted out every waking period of Koyil's tortuous life. A mass of material was stored away in their immediate consciousness. And one unspeakable fact was laid bare, look away from it as they would.

Koyil had studied the Banned Weapons, outlawed in the almost-mythical times beyond the memory of any of their kind.

"It was tested on Argoyil, which was then a world just coming into flower." Neryi sighed, his eyes full of pain. "My people murdered, through uncaring ignorance, that young world, strangling it before it had emerged from the womb of time. It is now a barren rock, scarred and blackened by the fires that were loosed there. Worse, it is poisoned to the deeps of its rock with the breath of those ill-conceived weapons that my fathers' fathers wrought. They took the sun-fire and twisted it into death that flew and fell, death that crept as a fog through the air, death that could be hurled from a hand-held thing."

"But who were their enemies?" asked Yinri, her green eyes dark with foreboding.

"I told you once, long ago, that Hasyih raises up her own enemies. Those enemies are not real ones, merely dark phantoms that stalk inside the minds of some of our kind. Yet a part of our kindred have never learned to winnow out the false from the true. To them danger has always seemed a near and immediate thing. It was such who fathered the Banned Weapons. They fathered, also, Koyil and most of his fellows. A strain of madness runs through my kind, Yinri, thought not in my direct line. It has led to self-destruction for many—too many. For that reason, primarily, you found only six Children of the Asyi on guard in your realm, when you came. There should have been ten times our number here to greet you."

"Then you, with Amaryi and Anyi, Ziniyi and Lonyi and Eryi, are the last, save for those who cleave to Koyil?" she asked, laying her hand upon his arm. "Truly, we are outnumbered in this ill-sprung war."

Neryi looked down at her with great tenderness.

"Ah, no," he said. "We have the Queen Who Has Come Again. For this reason you were saved from the fall of your father's hold. For this reason you were given the lyre and led through the doorway into Hasyih. For this reason only, I dare to guess, Those Who Pattern the Worlds sent your father forth with Koyil in the beginning. In your hands is the fate not only of Hasyih but of all the contiguous worlds."

"But my only power came through the lyre!" she exclaimed. "I know so little, within myself!"

"Remember that you contain, as well as yourself, that other, older Yinri. Yet even she is not the most important thing to consider. You have been trained at the hands of the gods for this task."

She drew away from him, perched upon the edge of the flat slab of the table and tapped her foot upon the floor, excitement kindling in her eyes.

"Do you remember when Arbold and Enid came through from Ranuit?" she asked him, and he nodded. "You said that below in the tower were terrible weapons that only the Children of the Asyi—and I—could approach. Are those the Banned Weapons?"

Reluctantly he nodded again.

"Could they be used to defend our land and our people against Koyil?"

He sighed. She was so much a child, at times; he was wont to forget that in her amazing strength and maturity at others. Sixteen short years cannot instill very much of balanced judgment, no matter what the charac-

er and the training. He rose and moved to stand at her
ide, looking down into her eyes.

"Think, Yinri. If you use such weapons in Hasyih
. . then Hasyih will die horribly, every person, every
ree, every blade of grass. Never to live again, perhaps.
To lie burned and shattered like Argoyil. And Hasyih
s the Heart of the Worlds. What happens here must
ind an echo in every world that touches upon this."

Her face sobered, and she, in turn, nodded slowly.

"Now think again. If you send them through into
Ranuit, then that world will die, instead of Hasyih. All
ts folk, and they are many, I have learned from Arbold
ind Enid, will come to a dreadful ending. To make an
:nd to Koyil, the thing would have to be done by stealth
ind without waiting or warning. Could we do such a
:hing, even to save Hasyih?"

"No. Of course we could not. Better to suffer and
to die than to inflict suffering and death," was her instant
reply. "Yet I would save this world, if it can be done
honorably and without peril to those who are innocent
and unknowing."

"You, Love, are the rock that looms in Koyil's path.
The gods have set you here for that purpose. Wait. The
way will be laid clearly before us," he replied.

IX

Chilled and stiff, Inyit rose from his inadequate
shelter. Night again crept over the horizon of Hasyih,
hurried on by the still-steady rain. Though there was still

a bit of light in the sky, the spy felt secure in setting out at once. None, he knew, would be abroad in the winter fields that now lay before him, sodden and stubble-laden.

And when the first hem of paler sky lay again across the east, Inyit stood beneath the very wall of the City. He knew that no eye had seen his wet journey. Deep within himself, he felt a wariness, an unease. There was an intuition that someone within the walls had known, without seeing, that he was abroad. Still, he had accepted for too long Koyil's skepticism. His belief in the eyes of the spirit was eroded away, and he dismissed his own sure instinct.

Finding the bulk of the tower against the lightening sky, he paced to his left, counting. When he had measured off a quarter of the circle that bounded the City, he stood against the streaming stone and whispered, "Ilyisit nohoryim."

There came a dim grinding, a grating of stone against stone, and he smelled the dusty and unbreathed air of a passage that now stood open to receive him. Feeling a quiet triumph, he stepped into the wall and heard the door close behind him. The way was possible. Koyil could, indeed, set his weapons within the very wall of the City, when the time was right.

X

Guyin stood in the forest. About him great bells of blossom drooped on loops of vine, swinging in the morning breeze to loose their potent scents into the air. Though he had caught a glimpse of autumn as he stepped upon the soil of the other continent, this more southerly one knew nothing of that season. Its jungle, changing from moment to moment, was the same from year's end to year's end.

It was still early, and the steamy heat that would build with the day had not yet descended. In the freshness of the new day, the branches above him were alive with living creatures, some returning from their night's hunting, others just beginning their activities.

On impulse, he reached up, caught a low-hung branch, and swung himself into the nearest tree. Not since boyhood had he so indulged his whims, and he chuckled as he climbed higher, gripping the shapes of the limbs with his soft-shod feet as he reached for new handholds.

The lawful tenants of the tree made room for him peaceably, and he went up and up into the tremendous growth, finding himself at last upon a perch just beneath the stiff-leaved green crown. The jungle surged away on three sides like a static sea, and on the fourth side the precise pattern of the Folkplace lay, round and gemlike, as if it were a dream or a mirage.

Guyin sat upon the convenient branch and looked down, watching the tiny figures that were the folk as they moved along the moss-green pathways, splashed in the silver-glinting pools, or went away into the forest upon their daily tasks. For the first time in many weeks, he found his heart at ease. The waiting, which should have been no task to his kind, had ground upon his spirit. Mnemora and her people, short-lived though they were, had known less impatience than had he, whose age must be measured against that of the planet rather than its inhabitants.

The morning breeze, thick with the odor of leaf and bloom, beast and decaying vegetation, moved against his cheek. He turned his head to gaze away across the low-lying forest to his left, but a distant voice called his attention back toward the Folkplace.

Not often did the folk of the forest continent have need to call aloud. Among themselves, they were so closely interconnected, mind to mind, that speech was a seldom-used thing. But Guyin had closed away that part of his heritage, at Koyil's behest, and it was opening again only slowly. So they called his name upon the wind of morning, and he fled down the tree and toward the caller.

He found Mnemora and Aloye waiting. Their tranquility was unruffled, their eyes deep and quiet; yet he felt as he neared them a subtle tension that had not been a part of them before. It was as though a flame of invisible energy were now burning behind their still faces, lighting the air about them with preternatural brightness.

"Koyil moves," said Mnemora, turning her coppery face up to him. "Things walk in the wind; time turns on its spindle; and we must now take thought to our own actions."

"I will get the lyre," answered the blue-clad minstrel, but Aloye silently bent over and lifted the instrument from the shelter of a creamy-flowered bush.

It was glinting fiercely in the clean wash of sunlight, its greenbone frame glowing as if with an inner brilliance, its strings shimmering silver. When it reached Guyin's hands, it glowed brighter yet, and a hum, as if of anticipation, filled the air.

"Who goes with me?" asked Guyin. The two who stood beside him nodded and stepped close.

His hands caressed the lyre, and notes sprang angrily into the air. They were so infinitely bright that they paled even the newly risen sun, and they patterned themselves in the air, forming a shape of fire. As note was added to note in a fierce and intricate melody, a structure was limned in brilliance before the three.

Mnemora and Aloye watched, eyes wide and wondering, as a doorway shaped itself for their use. And it was no simple arch, such as Guyin had used before. It was fretted with tendrils of silver flame, studded with gems of angry color. It was wide enough for three abreast to walk through with ease.

As one, they moved forward and stepped through the glowing portal.

XI

Once again the tower pulsed with deep-hidden power. In their restored chamber, high in its smooth shape, Koyil and his people were at work. Yet there was a difference.

Koyil, driven as ever by his obsessions, did the work of three . . . or, now, four. For his fellows' hearts were at odds with their hands, as they labored to make the destruction of their home-world. In the intricate process that they now pursued, this made for slowness, indeed.

The mechanisms that lay on their worktables were small, true, but they were the vital nerve systems of the weapons that they had formed to channel the sun-fire's fury. There were too few of them to risk any life in triggering those terrible things. So Koyil, out of the deeps of his madness and anger, had designed devices that, upon a subtle signal, would loose the poisoned power of his weapons upon Hasyih.

Inyit, stooped over his task, felt his inward parts cringe at the thing he was about to assist in doing. The air of Hasyih had been sweet with old memories. Even the rain had fallen upon his skin like the caress of a lost lover. The wet-stone scent of the City's wall, the musty gloom of the secret way had been signals to rouse a long-forgotten part of him. His spirit cringed at the thought of that sweet land going down into the dust and desolation that now enwrapped Argoyil. But he worked on, flogging his hands to do their duty, let his secret self rebel as it would.

They had labored for days upon these little messengers of death. Though Koyil had fretted and his temper had often boiled up, he had not succeeded in speeding the process; but now, let the Hasyisi be as reluctant as they would, the thing was all but done. The minute testing that Inyit had insisted was necessary had been completed. The inward parts were placed and secured. Now the covers were being sealed into place. The time was upon them, for good or ill.

When the last of the four devices was ready, the golden-eyed tyrant of their lives gazed upon his folk, and even they cringed at the thing they saw in his face.

"Inyit, take three and bring out the weapons, one by one, laying them to north and south, east and west of the tower, keeping its bulk between them."

Inyit bowed his head, turned on his heel, and, gesturing to three of his kindred, went down into the deeps where those unholy things lay, gently breathing their poison into the stone on which they rested. They were heavy, for they were shielded with gray metal and impregnated cloths, but the four managed to bring them, one by one, to their appointed places.

When all were laid in the light of the late fall day, Koyil himself attached the triggering devices, trusting not even his own to do it with the necessary precision. Then he stood and looked at his kin once more.

"You have been given your instructions. Each pair has in it one who has walked the ways recently. The keys are within your minds. It only remains to act, my brothers and sisters. This day's work, well done, will wreak vengeance for terrible wrongs and deep injustices. Go, and fare you well." He turned on his heel and re-entered the tower.

The twenty Hasyisi left beside the tower gazed upon one another for a long moment. Their closed faces betrayed no hint of the things their hearts were feeling, and no word now passed between any of them. Then, by two and by two, eight of them moved away from their peers, toward their waiting tasks.

Inyit, paired with Syina, his wife of long standing, heard the click of their heels upon the old stone as if from a great distance. The sun burned through their heavy cloaks, chosen for the winter that had raged in Hasyih when he and the other spies had last walked there. The dull lump that was their weapon lay beside the tower; but even swaddled as it was, it hinted at terrible things.

He bent beside Syina, and they lifted together, then laid the thing upon the light, wheeled carrier they had devised for the transporting of the heavy burdens. Then, in the brightness of Ranuit's pale sun, they spoke together.

The doorway opened before them, and they pulled the cart through into a wild and blustery afternoon upon the side of a mountain, facing, once again, the southern forest.

The Rune
of Endings

I

THE DOORWAY that the lyre had opened led Guyin and his companions directly into one of the small gardens that studded the City. Though it was sodden with rain, its blossoms and leafage winter-killed, its design was poignantly familiar to the minstrel, who stopped in his tracks to look about him. The stone-flagged paths radiated from the central fountain in colorful patterns of mosaic. The wistful figures of white granite stood peering shyly through the leafless shrubbery, even as they had done when he played there as a child. The scent of wet soil and soaked piles of dead leaves was winy in his nostrils. He was home, after eons.

Mnemora and the boy stood quietly, letting him drink his fill of memory. Then she touched his arm, and he smiled down at her.

"You are right," he said. "Now we must go to the Queen—my child, strange as that may seem—and tell her of her peril. May we be led well, Lady, for if not this graceful world will die."

They went through the mist of rain, but strangely enough it seemed neither to cling to nor even to touch any of them. When they arrived at the tower steps, their robes were lightly moving about them. The lyre was gleaming like a little sun; and where its bubble of light ran, the rain did not fall.

The guard who stood at the deep doorway of the

tower saw them as they came. Before they began to mount the steps, they heard the clamor of a deep-throated bell, high above them. And when they saw the door begin to swing open, its heavy leaves moving apart as they approached, they knew that the lyre had broadcast their arrival, perhaps even as they came through the gateway of light.

They went into the hall as four figures came down the stair from the upper reaches of the Tower. The foremost was a tall young woman clad in a full-cut green robe that fluttered in the wake of her swift motion. Behind her was a square, golden-eyed man who was, without doubt, one of Guyin's kindred. And last of all came a man and a woman, both of middle-age, both scarred and marked by time and hardships.

Guyin stopped where he stood, and Mnemora and Aloye halted on either hand. Lifting the lyre high, Guyin waited as the four approached. Then he set it beside his foot and bowed.

"We have come, Queen of Hasyih, with warning . . . and, perhaps, with some small aid. Peril walks out of Ranuit into your lands, and we come a bit before."

Yinri bent and lifted the lyre. It seemed to shine with even greater brightness as her hand touched it, but she was looking at the smooth curve of its frame.

"When first I took this lyre from the willow tree, its frame was unmarked. Now, see, Neryi, there are four runes. The rune of the key, there at the top. Then the rune of weaponry. Questions unanswered. Questions answered. And there is space for one more. What will it be, I wonder?"

Neryi sighed. "It will be either the rune of beginnings—or that of endings, my love. But now we must take council with our guests, for they have much to tell us."

He bowed his head to Guyin, making the sign of greeting reserved for the Children of the Asyi. "Welcome, kinsman and companion of my ancestors," he said. "Never in my waking life had I thought to meet your living self." Then he offered his hands, first to Mnemora, then to Aloye.

When all were settled once again in the chamber nearby, and the demands of hospitality were met, Guyin settled himself into a deep chair and said, "Firstly, let me provide a strange, though not unpleasant, surprise. Yinri, Queen of Hasyih, you see before you your father, Guyin, who unwisely followed Koyil into exile." He smiled, for the faces of the four before him were full of interest and speculation.

"I went for the sake of Inyis; and when she was no more, I took myself away among the people of Ranuit. I woke and slept many times. Then I met your mother, Yinri, and you were born. For a short time my long life seemed worth enduring. Then came the attack . . . and I died. Truly died. But Those Who Pattern the Worlds set me in a place where time and body and action did not exist. Only expiation, thought, and memory lived there. The note of the lyre brought me forth in a new flesh, and I am wiser than I was before.

"The lyre led me through two doors, one into the continent of your birth, where I took its shape into my hand, and the second into the forest continent across the seas. There I was taught what had occurred in the time of my death. Mnemora and her folk had followed all, keeping every fact in perspective and using their great gifts to foresee much of what must come. Even across those dimensions, they followed Enid and Arbold, so that we knew you were aware of the threat of Koyil. They knew they were helpless to interfere, for their bodies cannot cross the thresholds . . . and then I came with the lyre. My function was just this—to open a way for Mnemora and her helper to cross into this dimension.

"Now we come with a terrible word. Koyil is moving against Hasyih, using the Banned Weapons. She cannot tell exactly when or where he will strike, but it will be soon and very near. She and Aloye bring within them the potencies of all their people. When they link into any defense we contrive, tremendous power will accompany them."

Yinri rose and came to kneel beside him. "I am twice blessed," she said, "for I have been given two fathers. Together we will triumph, if it can be done honorably, or we will fail and die together."

II

The tower was still with waiting. Koyil stood in his high chamber, and with him were Inyit and Syina and all who had gone forth into Hasyih and all who had been left behind. Upon the reconstructed panels were patterns of light that, beneath Koyil's skilled hands, were settling into forms that woke longing in the hearts of his comrades. For with the weapons that had been taken into Hasyih had gone perceptors capable of conveying impulses across the dimensions. Koyil intended to see the death of Hasyih.

When the pictured places had steadied, he turned his attention to the small mechanism that lay before him on his stone-faced table. It bore two small buttons upon its red case, one large green one and one smaller golden one. When their leader took this up, all the Hasyisi in the chamber breathed a deep sigh.

In that moment, though their flesh remained, as always, faithful and obedient, their spirits closed themselves away from Koyil and his purpose. Intent upon his task, he noticed nothing as he depressed the green button.

A zigzag of interruption marked the panels as energies moved from world to world, alerting the devices that would trigger the weapons. Koyil smiled grimly and looked up at the waiting faces about him. But he did not really see them. He saw only his own heart's fury and vengeance mirrored there, and that satisfied his concern.

With his thumb he slowly touched the golden button.

III

Guyin stood with his daughter and her husband, Arbold and Enid, Mnemora and Aloye upon the parapet at the top of the tower. In his hands was the lyre, shining its green light into the gloomy day. Something of that effulgent greenness enwrapped them all, glowing from the air about them. Yinri's eyes shone almost as brightly as the instrument, and her face was alive with concentrated power.

All save Guyin were linked, hand to hand. Into that linkage was flowing concentrated energies that came from many sources: Those who sat below in the temple; those who remained in their homes in the City but poured their thought into the task at hand; the Children of the Asyi; and those who dwelled across the dimensions in Ranuit, whose powerful willing was felt by every link in that chain.

The Weapons had been placed, each of them knew. Where to seek them was a futile question, for at any moment they would be triggered. Only the power of Those Who Pattern the Worlds might be a defense against such infinitely destructive things, and that power was locked into the lyre.

Key and weapon, question and answer, the lyre held potencies that had never before been combined and channeled. As Koyil touched the golden button, the lyre pulsed with unbearable brilliance, and Guyin struck the strings into one mind-shattering chord.

The world rocked about them. The tower creaked and groaned. Bits of stone and slate clattered down into the street below, as the sky, so gray and forbidding a moment before, blossomed into fantastic brightness. They could see, in that eery light, the trees at the edge of the tilled lands burst into flame that ran away across the grasslands in one vast sheet of fire.

Then came wind, sweeping down into the space about the City, carrying the fires high in spiraling gouts that were lost in the dust and smoke that ensued. But the Ctiy stood, untouched save by that first shock.

Over it, from wall face to wall face, a shimmering green bubble rose. Against it the blast had been powerless, the fires impotent, the winds harmless. Pure force, formed by human and nonhuman wills, it was impervious to such weaponry.

Safe within the City was every Hasyisi who could be found and saved. Few of Yinri's folk had been left to perish, only those who had been too far to find. Yet, having saved the people, those upon the tower had been powerless to save their lands, for the mountains lay shattered, the forests burned away, and fields and pastures poisoned with the breath of the Banned Weapons.

Seeing afar with their inner senses, Yinri and Neryi stood upon the tower and wept for the loveliness that had been Hasyih. Guyin felt their grief and loss, but he was older by far than even Neryi, and he had lost too much, too many times, to waste himself in sorrow.

"Now we must go out," he said. "There are other continents, rich and productive, that have lain waiting for our feet, the touch of the plow, the work of the tonecutter. Our folk have wasted millennia in this graceful land, for it was too comfortable to leave. Now they must leave while there is force left in the lyre to shelter their journey. That must be our task, Queen of the World."

Yinri bowed her head. No trace of the soft young girl who had lifted down the lyre remained to her. She was now, in full truth, a queen well fitted to lead her people into a new life. But she did not think, just yet, of her tremendous task.

"How fared Ranuit?" she asked Mnemora, turning to look down into the woman's bright face.

"The sun is obscured; the land trembled deeply. No tree fell, and the waters still run clear. It is safe, Lady, my folk believe," she answered.

"But those in that other tower—" her listeners were intent upon her words—"stand frozen in their places. A bubble of force, much like this about us, surrounds that tower and its circling city. None moves within, nor can move. Koyil and his folk are imprisoned until Those Who Pattern the Worlds see fit to release them."

IV

The willow rustled, its gray-tan leaves dropping into the stream below. The sun, low in the south, gilded the little beach, the flat rock, the stiff brown remnants of the reeds. Only the wind hummed there, singing through dead leafage and stalks. One late grasshopper zinged plaintively in the wood.

A rook swept over the willow, its shadow flicking across the ripples of the stream. Then it rose high to clear the forest and flew away across the forests and fields, and its lonely cry came down the wind to those who made ready for winter.

Epilogue

THE NEW CITY was rising. It was no less beautiful than the old city, though it was by necessity built of other materials and in less time-consuming fashion. Still, the Hasyisi could build no otherwise than beautifully.

Yinri sat on a stone, watching the keystone set into the entrance to the new temple. This temple, she devoutly hoped, would never be defiled, as the other had been. Her green eyes noted every move of the masons, and she smiled a secret smile to see her husband lend his hand to passing up the mortar to the master mason, who for this time was more important to his people even than Neryi of the Asyi.

The tree that drooped above her seat dropped a golden petal. It settled on the cheek of the child in her lap, and a pair of eyes as green as Yinri's own opened in astonishment. The rosy lips opened, too and a questioning, "Ahhh-maa?" brought her mother's gaze downward.

The smile grew wider. Yinri lifted the warm bundle and cuddled her face into the baby's middle. Chuckles quivered against her nose, and she set young Aryi against her shoulder and rocked herself slowly.

It had seemed hard, all those months ago, to leave the land that was the only one her people had ever known. They were frightened and, though new things were all that her own experience had ever held, that had fright-

ened her a bit. Yet her father Guyin, before going into
his last sleep, had told her many useful things about the
management of her people. And her father Arbold had
been a rock and a staff, solving problems of transport, of
moving and feeding a multitude, and of settling them
into a new land with the ease of an old hand at such tasks.

He and Enid had become, to the Hasyisi and to the
Children of the Asyi, almost revered figures. Their
counsel was sought after in emergencies. Their tough
wisdom had circumvented many a potential problem.
And their simple presence had bolstered the strength and
confidence of both Yinri and Neryi. They had lived
through far worse things than this. It was written on
their faces. It was implicit in their words and actions.
The knowledge that they had done so and survived was
a reassuring thing to the people who had survived the
wreck of Hasyih.

Now the new life was shaping itself before Yinri's
eyes. Fields were tilled and planted, and young green had
already covered the dark soil with its freshness. The
short-lived ones, shaken to their roots by the catastrophe
they had survived by so scanty a margin, had lost their
resentment of the Children of the Asyi and worked beside them in fair amity.

The King had lost his plump and lazy facade, turning
his mind and his hands to creating a life that could be
even better than he had known before. Even those who
had secretly scoffed at the old traditions of their people
had been convinced of the truth when that devastating
force had dashed itself, futilely, against the bubble that

the Asyi, Yinri, her two fathers, Enid, and the people from Ranuit had raised above them.

The temple would be finished before winter. It would be a winter far more severe than those the Hasyisi had known before. Here no protecting mountains rose about to shelter the city from the winds. The subterranean ducts that had brought warmth into the houses from beneath the soil could not be built so quickly, and they must rely on the sun and fires from the thick forests that began beyond their fields. Still, none had grumbled at the thought of a winter of discomfort.

The master mason fitted the keystone into place, gave a last swipe of his trowel, and stepped back on his platform, allowing those below to see. The stone glowed with green glimmers in the sunlight. There was an "oooh!" of appreciation from the throng that had left their labors to watch this most important of endeavors.

Yinri lifted the baby and turned her. "See, Aryi? See the portal? In years to come, you will walk through that doorway many times. I wonder if you could possibly remember seeing it, fresh and new?"

Aryi cooed and waved her little fists, seeing her father on the platform.

The master mason, feeling that some gesture from him would be fitting, bowed low in their direction.

"To the Queen Who Has Come," he cried, and his voice echoed away among the half-built walls and towers of the new city.

"And to the little Queen Who Is to Come!"

Yinri rose and bowed in return. The child crowed

loudly, and all there, from the masons to Arbold to Neryi, himself, broke into laughter. Then they turned away, each to his own task, leaving Yinri to muse beneath the golden willow.